THE NEW BIZARRO AUTHOR SERIES

PRESENTS

LOVE IN THE TIME OF DINOSAURS

I0630241

KIRSTEN ALENE

Eraserhead Press
Portland, OR

THE NEW BIZARRO AUTHOR SERIES
An Imprint of Eraserhead Press

ERASERHEAD PRESS
205 NE BRYANT
PORTLAND, OR 97211

WWW.ERASERHEADPRESS.COM

ISBN: 1-936383-24-1

You hold in your hands now a book from the New Bizarro Author Series. Normally, Eraserhead Press publishes twelve books a year. Of those, only one or two are by new writers. The NBAS alters this dynamic, thus giving more authors of weird fiction a chance at publication.

For every book published in this series, the following will be true: This is the author's first published book. We're testing the waters to see if this author can find a readership, and whether or not you see more Eraserhead Press titles from this author is up to you.

If enough copies of this book aren't sold within a year, there will be no future books from the author published by Eraserhead Press. So, if you enjoy this author's work and want to see more in print, we encourage you to help her out by writing reviews of his book, telling your friends, and giving feedback at www.bizarrocentral.com.

In any event, hope you enjoy...

—Kevin L. Donihe, Editor

For Cameron and Dad

Prologue
The Myth of the Great Destroyer

At the center of the planet, which is as wide in circumference as one thousand birds flying consecutively from birth to exhaustion, there is a vast, empty cavern, and in that cavern there are forty floating islands which circle each other slowly, propelled by the vibrations of footsteps falling on the surface of the earth.

On each island live an old woman and an old man. Each old woman is unaware of the presence of the old man, and each old man is unaware of the presence of the old woman.

They have been eighty-seven years old since time began. They sleep on the boughs of trees and are wakened each morning by a sun-streak across the sky, like a giant fluorescent light bulb made of the fireflies that orbits each floating island.

At the End of Days—when the islands break free from the cavernous center of the planet and burst into the light of day, the old women and the old men on the islands will find each other and, in ecstasy at the discovery of another human, will mate with the fireflies. Their offspring will be the only thing that can stop Jeremy.

Jeremy: the scourge of mankind, the Great Destroyer.

Chapter One
Raptor Reconnaissance

Oomka fidgets beside me. He wipes sweat from his brow, smearing the painted camouflage patches and exposing a swatch of pink skin. I'm trying to use this time to catch up on some meditation and steady my hands a bit, but it's hard to meditate beside Oomka. He fidgets too much. Still, it's not like meditating will do me any good. All that comes to me in meditation lately is the story of the Great Destroyer. And Jeremy. Thinking about Jeremy makes me even more anxious. It's understandable, considering the circumstances.

* * *

In the last twenty-five years, *Jeremy* has taken on a whole new meaning. Before then, a monk in the monastery would have heard the word only once in a while—whenever the community was unlucky enough to be visited by a man-eating tiger, or someone discovered a snake in the public bathroom. Someone might scream, "Ah! Jeremy! Back, Jeremy!" as he ran from the toilet, or "Ah! Look out, a Jer…" before being eaten by a tiger.

Prior to the End of Days, The Myth of the Great Destroyer, the shortest section in the *Book of Meditation*, provided the only knowledge anyone had about Jeremies. Since then, hundreds of books have been written about them, totaling more than one million pages of data, observation, speculation and statistics.

For all that work, all the lives sacrificed in the name of research, and all the slaughter and loss and pain, no one knows where they come from, what they want, or how to defeat them.

What we have gathered is this: Jeremies are dinosaurs,

primarily from the Cretaceous period. There are fourteen known varieties, although my dead friend Chip suspected there were more that we've just never seen up close. He had good reason to believe this, and I have no reason to doubt him, as he is currently in the third stomach of some Jeremy cast in plastic about seven miles north of the monastery wall.

In addition to the obvious biological advantage of being dinosaurs, Jeremies are unfairly favored in the fight. Their technology far surpasses ours; their hand-to-hand combat skills are uncanny and they all, without exception, have an insatiable lust for human blood.

The only advantage we seem to possess is our unique connection to and familiarity with our surroundings (mountain forests where the majority of us have spent our entire lives). But guerilla warfare is as taxing as our temple duties and rituals, and coping with our spiritual imprisonment and the constant onslaught of the Jeremy is too much for many of the monks. In the last two years alone, we've lost more than eighty men.

This figure, of course, excludes the countless villagers that have fallen victim to the Jeremy whenever they break through our safe lines.

* * *

Oomka trembles beside me as I struggle to remain in the state of transcendent calm I usually occupy during watch duty. Sure, Jeremies scare the living shit out of me. But what's the use of being a monk if you can't transcend your physical existence when faced with the imminent death of your species?

Of everyone in the monastery, aside from the two elders, I am perhaps the most familiar with the fourteen known varieties of Jeremy. From as early as I can remember, books concerning the Jeremy have fascinated me. Their biology, their technology, their strategy, their tight-knit cooperative communities, their language and intelligent thought are a source of continual amazement and wonder.

I can't help but look at them with reverent, even worshipful eyes. From their perfect rows of bone crushing, razor-sharp teeth to the arched, reptilian spines that allow them to navigate at top speeds through any terrain, every movement, every expression is carefully measured, agile, streamlined and sensual. Especially when compared with the pathetic scrambling movements of the monks and villagers.

To watch them hunt, to see them bring down a human in battle, demands a sort of awful silence of mind. Those who can't find in themselves a cool, observant respect for the creatures don't last long.

* * *

"Look," Oomka whispers in my ear, gesturing with shaking hands through the heavy cover of our tree down to the forest floor. There is a rustle of movement, barely perceivable. Could be anything.

A squirrel.

Or a badger.

Then I hear a high, rapid clicking call.

Raptors.

My body tenses. I aim the ray gun downward and wait for another rustle. Fortunately for us, raptors are shit at climbing, and Oomka and I, as usual, have chosen a tall tree with sparse lower branches, good as a vantage point, but a huge risk as an attack position. I always bank on the sight-advantage giving us ample warning time to descend if an attack comes.

I catch a flash of light from a tree opposite ours, across the ravine. One of the other watch pairs has seen the movement as well. I nudge Oomka and gesture to the mirror signal. Probably more than one raptor, which usually means an attack party. I wait for the undergrowth to shift again. It'd be best to encase these two (or more) Jeremies before descending. Oomka shudders as he aims his gun down at the same spot of undergrowth.

But I plunge my mind into the spongy vat of comfort conjured up from the depths of my being, and my movements become automatic and graceful. I swing the ray gun around, flashing the glass sight so the other team knows what I'm about to do. I wave two fingers at Oomka, and he steadies his gun against his knee.

The raptor nearest us has popped up its head in a clear section of forest floor. It swivels around slowly, face tilted to the side, listening. It has tremendous auditory senses and can probably hear our breaths, our heart beats, the blinking of our eyelids, the creaking of our bones, Oomka's pores squeezing out miniscule drops of perspiration, our sticky hands sliding over the barrels of the guns. It just can't see us.

In the same second, Oomka and I fire our guns. I hit my target, but Oomka misses by a fraction of an inch. My raptor has been encased in hard, flesh-colored plastic, his last scream still echoing through the ravine. The other raptor has wisely put its head down and disappeared into the brush.

Two more shots ricochet off the trees from the other watch team.

As their gun blasts echo, and we sweep the undergrowth for movement, a massive cavern of teeth explodes out of the trees directly behind us. With a moaning exhalation of putrid, meat-smelling breath, the mountainous jaws of a brachiosaurus clamp down on Oomka's lower half.

I yell and swing my ray gun around, but it is too late. The monster has withdrawn into the leaves, taking the bottom half of Oomka with it. The top half of Oomka looks at me, his yellow eyes bulging as fluid and blood pour from the remaining half of his torso. Two exposed ribs dangle below a line of jagged flesh. Organs spill out over the tree limb, coating the branches beneath us in vivid red. He coughs, and a mouthful of blood trickles down his chin, staining the front of his orange robes. He still clutches one of the tree limbs directly above us, but has dropped his gun. It lies half-obscured in the brush below us.

"Oomka?" I say, half-pitying, half-disgusted.

Often I have wished that we were stronger, bigger and more lethal without the aid of our tools, machines and weapons, which barely compensate for our lack of teeth and claws. Born weak and naked into this world, we are helpless. I want to rip into the leathery flesh of the dinosaurs. I want sharp teeth. I want to tear into Jeremies, to disembowel them with my bare hands, to bite them in half and feast on their cold-blooded flesh.

When the dinosaurs first appeared, the elders forbade violence against them. But the number of deaths spiraled out of control. Villagers were devoured, and the constant carnage forced us into action. We had no choice but to defend what was ours—our monastery, our villages, our mountain—from destruction and death.

When the elders decided to act, finally, they armed us with ray guns that did not kill Jeremies instantly, but encased their bodies in hard plastic. Somehow, this was thought to be more humane.

* * *

There's still hope for Oomka. If I can get him back to the monastery, the physicians will be able to fit him with another lower body, and he'll be back on someone else's feet and fighting in no time. The magic kung-fu of the monks, learned from the venerable Elder Zohar—one of the last surviving elders of the monastery—combined with the impressive skills of our physicians, have led to many astounding recoveries that would have been impossible for the monks to achieve twenty years ago. The only things that can destroy us are complete obliteration or ritual self-destruction. But our watch isn't over for another three hours, and it looks like a fight is coming.

"Are you alright?" I ask, shifting my ray gun onto my back so I can climb down to retrieve his gun before more Jeremies show up. Those two raptors were just advance scouts, and one probably made it back to the attack party. The worst is yet to come. And they know our positions.

"Well, yeah," Oomka says matter-of-factly, running a finger around the torn flesh of his lower chest, picking a few leaves off the shredded muscle tissue. "Go get the gun. I can hang here. But when you come back up, I'm gonna ask you to shift me a little. I think I'm resting on my spine, and I can't see very well."

He's acting strangely. It annoys me that he'd let a thing like this get to him, but I can't say anything negative while he's in this state.

"No problem," I say, sliding down onto the next lowest branch, which is slick with Oomka's blood and what looks like some intestine.

By the time I've retrieved the ray gun and clambered back into position, Oomka is still not quite himself. It's a big shock to lose half of your body, of course, but it's not the end of the world. Oomka seems to have taken it pretty hard. I think that if it'd been me, I'd have handled the situation better.

With my half-functional, distracted partner I feel more vulnerable and exposed, so I plunge my mind back into the elastic receptacle of peace I've manifested, isolating each functional part of my body, cooling my blood as it races through my veins, flexing each finger separately, bending each hair toward the sun like blades of grass to absorb the green light filtered through the canopy of leaves above us.

It'll be fine, I reassure myself silently, wondering if Oomka is going to have my back at all. He's still inspecting the ragged flesh of his torso, picking at it.

"Don't do that," I tell him.

"Yeah, I know," he says, but he doesn't stop.

* * *

Oomka and I have only known each other for a few months. Until recently, I'd really disliked him, but we spend a lot of time together on watch duty and patrolling the outer wall, so we've become rather close. We've gotten used to each other, and I've begun to trust him.

It was difficult to take on another partner for watch duty after my previous partner, my best and oldest friend, Chip, was dismembered and eaten by a stegosaurus. Chip was the sort of man who was always present in the moment. I strove to be like him in almost every way. I still do.

When he was dismembered, he sacrificed himself to allow the others and me to get back to the walls of the monastery. If he hadn't dove into that hopeless engagement with the stegosaurus, all seven of us would have died. He had lived for the utility of his every move until his very last second on earth.

But the one aspect of Chip's worldview I never agreed with was his bitter, unbridled loathing of the Jeremy. He hated them to such a degree that he failed to accept or anticipate their ingenuity and intelligence. He was blinded by anger and rage, and no matter how noble his sacrifice had been, it eventually cost him his life.

As the elders taught us, only with respect, careful, minute observation, and unfailing strength of body and mind would we be able to hold out against our enemy. *Hold Out*. For, as I constantly reminded myself, we held no advantage. We had no hope. In the end, we were children.

* * *

Oomka fidgets nervously with the settings on his ray gun now, turning the plastic-thickness knob up and down and gazing through the crosshairs, aiming at trees and shrubs.

This is one of the reasons why I initially disliked Oomka.

He fidgets. Chip never fidgeted. He could sit on watch duty like a stone, in one position for the entire five-hour shift. What I wouldn't give to be as centered and calm as Chip had been.

Although I don't twitch and fidget as much as Oomka, I find myself having to change position often, especially straddling this tree limb. My genitals are pinned uncomfortably against the joint of a branch extending from the larger limb we sit on, and no amount of repositioning will make it comfortable. I'm almost envious of Oomka's lack of genitals, but then I figure it's probably just as uncomfortable resting on one of your own exposed ribs.

* * *

Our watch is almost over, and I feel the tension in my muscles releasing. The attack hasn't come. The brachiosaurus had simply been an unfortunate coincidence. Brachiosaurs often attacked at random. Few survive crossing their path.

The raptors weren't armed. But all the same, it makes me anxious to leave our watch so soon after that encasing, especially considering the raptor that got away.

I scan the forest floor below, looking for any sign of movement, any hint of an impending onslaught: a rustle in the ferns, the silence of birds, the sticky smell of raw meat on the breeze. There's nothing out of the ordinary.

But a flash from the adjacent watch makes Oomka and me jump. The movement of our bodies jostles the tree limb. Leaves at the end of the branch shudder, betraying our position to whatever the other watch may have spotted. I place a hand on Oomka's remaining chest to steady him, my body rigid, gun in hand and poised to shoot.

Then a scream rends the air, and we watch as a body plummets from the other watch position, falling into three even chunks in its descent. Blood cascades from the severed pieces, splattering like wet paint over the undergrowth. The mid-torso section bounces as it hits the earth.

Three round steel blades land in a tree several feet from our own, having crossed the ravine in less time than it took the body of our comrade to fall from its watch position.

Then, in a rush of instantaneous, synchronized movement, a mass of Jeremies clears the crest of the distant hill. Among them, brachiosaurs and tyrannosaurs tower above the heads of the other legions. The tyrannosaurs carry huge, triple-barreled bazookas with badger-sized torpedoes slung across their massive reptilian chests. Enormous jaws roar open and wide for imminent gnashing. Huge tails whip back and forth behind them, spiked with artificial barbs that impale ferns and small animals scurrying from the undergrowth away from the sprinting hordes.

The second watchman across the ravine tumbles through branches and lands broken on the ground below as two stegosaurs with a giant rotating saw held horizontally between them cut down his tree.

The sky explodes with smoke and ash as a torpedo from a nearby tyrannosaurus sends the body flying in fist-sized chunks up into the air.

He would have probably survived the fall. Unfortunately, the Jeremies had caught on to the fact that the monks weren't easy to kill, and desecrating and obliterating corpses had become one of their favorite pastimes.

I look at Oomka. Rivers of sweat streaking his camouflage face paint and mounting panic in his eyes tell me he's thinking what I'm thinking: without legs, in a ground battle, he doesn't stand a chance. I can hear Chip in my mind, as if he's yelling from a great distance, as if he's here in the moment with us, but standing far away, "Save yourselves! Back to the wall, go go go!"

And I know Oomka isn't that brave.

And I know I can't leave him to be slaughtered.

Our only chance is escape, to flee now as the blades and bullets fly past our tree, shredding leaves and splintering branches. The smell of raw meat, bleeding vegetation and gunpowder clouds my nostrils, filling my head with pressure. I can't think. We need time. But there is no time. Our present ammunition couldn't get us through this fight, even if every shot made contact (not an impossible feat when aiming at a virtually solid wall of Jeremies, but all the same). Oomka still trembles. Petrified, he stares at me. He isn't about to offer any suggestions. I'll have to come up with something.

My head whirrs around. I search desperately for an escape, willing a solution to come to me. The Jeremy attack force grows nearer, the scent of their filthy, meaty bodies intensifies, clouding my mind even more. I fling my eyes upward. Above the towering heads of the tyrannosaurs: a swarm of pterodactyls.

I duck a huge blade propelled by two large steam engines. It rips into the trunk of the tree behind our heads, cutting the top clean off. Our tree limb whips back. Oomka wedges his body into a more secure position, takes aim and fires at a brachiosaurus. The dinosaur is instantly coated in molten plastic, immobilized mid-stride. Smaller Jeremies leap out of the way of the blast. With sudden clarity, I bend over my ray gun and detach the shoulder strap. I swing the barrels up and aim into the swarm of pterodactyls.

Oomka plasticizes two smaller Jeremies with one shot and takes aim again. My shot has made contact, catching one pterodactyl full in the chest and splattering the wing of another. Both spiral to the forest floor. The Jeremy horde is at the bottom of the ravine, surging up the hill toward us, closing yards every second. The swarm of pterodactyls reacts exactly as I had hoped, rocketing toward us, enraged. They will beat the front lines to our tree, but just barely. Several more beaked bullets zip past us, burrowing their small, razor sharp faces into the flesh of the decapitated tree.

Oomka screams above the roar of the Jeremies: "What are you doing!?"

I gesture for him to shut up and spring onto the raw, severed neck of our tree. "Hold on to me!" I tell Oomka, "Don't let go!" He slings his weapon over his shoulder and grabs my ankle obediently.

"I'm going to swing you up!" I yell, gesturing to illustrate my intention. His eyes widen, but he doesn't argue. The pterodactyls, armed only with close-combat weapons and their own teeth, are nearing our position.

I brace myself on the treetop, hoping that Oomka's upper-half is light enough to fling into the air. He was never very heavy, even when he had legs. It has to work. It's our only chance.

The first pterodactyl dives through the leafy canopy toward us.

In one swift movement, I toss the ray gun strap. It winds around the Jeremy's jaw as I'd hoped, and I hurl Oomka's body, which is even lighter than anticipated, into the air. Oomka lands squarely on the pterodactyl and lowers a hand to pull me up. I yank the Jeremy down by its jaw and clamber up behind Oomka as quickly as possible. The other Jeremies, above and below, are upon us. A bullet rips through the pterodactyl's wing, making it falter and stumble in mid-flight.

"Go! Fly! NOW!" I yell, holding the ray gun against its scaly temple and shoving. My other hand is clenched tight around the strap binding its jaw. It obeys.

In seconds, we're tearing up into the sky, surrounded by other pterodactyls that swoop and dive at us. Their feet clasp long samurai swords that they clumsily slash through the air as they whirl around our injured pterodactyl, clicking and screeching.

Oomka aims the barrel of his ray gun under my arm and shoots a stream of flesh-colored plastic into the air. Pterodactyls avoid the blobs with angry screeches, but one of Oomka's shots makes contact. The plasticized pterodactyl plummets toward the forest below.

The other pterodactyls back away from our desperately

flapping prisoner. Several near the back of the swarm turn around to rejoin the battle raging below, probably to dive-bomb some other monks in watch posts in the trees. Overall, there are about forty monks out on watch. They should be able to handle the fight on the ground and retreat on foot to the walls of the monastery.

Once they reach the monastery, the attacking Jeremy horde will break upon the ancient, impenetrable stone walls like water.

But, as I look around, I see we're not anywhere near the monastery. In our haste, and surrounded by other pterodactyls, we must have flown in the wrong direction. The pterodactyl flaps its torn wing lamely. If it goes down now, we'll have to make our way back on foot outside the safe lines, with the attack force of Jeremy not far behind us.

Wet tears stream from the eyes of the pterodactyl. I feel an unwelcome surge of compassion and pity, and draw the ray gun back from its temple. Its body quakes feebly as its torn wing flaps at double speed under the extra weight of Oomka and me.

We still hear distant roaring and the frantic battle cries of monks on the ground. For a moment, I wish, bitterly, that I had stayed behind with them, but it would have meant sacrificing Oomka, a thing I couldn't bring myself to do. He aims the ray gun behind us, under my arm. Together, we sit on the pterodactyl in a sort of awkward, unintentional embrace, but it doesn't bother me.

The other pterodactyls have abandoned our trail, and the skies are clear ahead. Back toward the battle, a huge formation of cumulonimbus clouds amasses over the forest. Mingled with the smoke and steam and explosions tearing through the canopy of trees, the clouds look ominous.

I hope the monks on the ground will be able to subdue a large portion of the Jeremy attack force before they retreat to the walls. That would at least justify losing the monks who would die in today's firefight.

* * *

We are losing altitude fast. Treetops approach at an alarming rate, and nothing looks familiar. I yank up on the gun strap wound around the pterodactyl's beak, but its eyelids flicker. "Don't you dare die, you motherfucker!" I scream into the wind, jabbing the beast's side with my bare foot.

But the wings are folding; the pterodactyl spirals downward. I cling to the strap, but Oomka and I fall away from the pterodactyl. Oomka clutches the front of my robe like a baby possum, the remaining portion of his spinal column flapping beneath us in the roaring wind.

And we fall.

Our bodies shoot through the air toward the treetops. This is the end. The Jeremy is dead, or will be in a few seconds when it hits the ground. I feel a second surge of pity and compassion for the animal and try to shake this strange feeling from my head, not wanting to die mourning the fate of my enemy.

* * *

The green carpet racing up toward us, I close my eyes and dive into the folded fatty tissue of my brain. Swimming through electric impulses, curling around the stalks of neurons, I breaststroke through tissue toward the center. Like the planet, the center of my brain is an empty cavern. Shrill calls rend the air here. I wonder where they are coming from, but don't have time to look around. I have to reach my destination. There are no islands here, only an empty four-dimensional field. Corn grows along the center axis in neat rows. This is what I came for. The corn on the stalks is ripe. I pull the husk off greedily. The kernels are fireflies, buzzing and glowing in an even grid pattern. I take a huge bite, scraping the fireflies from the cob with my front teeth, a smile stretching over my face as I taste their buttery, luminous juices.

Suddenly, I realize where the shrill calls are coming from. Hungry pterodactyls race toward me as I drift aimlessly in the center of my brain. I know there's nothing I can do. I want to feed them the corn in my hands, so I lift it up to them, but they bite off my arms, and I scream in pain.

* * *

I am jerked out of my head. Oomka turns himself around so that his back is against my chest, and he rips open his ribcage. His hollow body cavity acts as a parachute, slowing our speed dramatically. We coast toward the trees and drop slowly through the canopy, unharmed. The remains of Oomka cushion my landing, and I roll away from him, sprawling out in the undergrowth. I close my eyes, relief rushing over my body like a tidal wave over a small village, obliterating houses and buildings and streets, and carrying every loose thing out to sea.

Chapter Three
Dinosaur Domicile

I prop myself up on an elbow and look around. I have no idea where we are. Oomka lies a few feet away, his ribcage open like a claw. There's nothing in his body cavity now. He's trying to prop himself up with his arms. I jump up and walk toward him. The pterodactyl is nowhere to be seen; we'll have to find our way back on foot.

Well, on my feet.

* * *

I am cleaning leaves out of my gun when I think I see a flash of movement about fifty yards away, a form darting through the trees several feet off the ground. It's hot and muggy in this part of the forest. Heat waves rise, distorting the shifting shapes. But, for some reason, my hands don't fly to the trigger of my gun. I don't even make a sign to Oomka to shut up. I just stare, waiting. And, in the bare yellow light streaking toward us from the edge of the forest, I think I see a lithe, slender body slip between two trees. I can't understand why my heart has leapt into my throat, or why I am trembling all over. I can't understand why my hands don't grasp my gun instinctively. I could have leveled the barrel, taken aim and fired. I should have fired. I should still fire. Cold sweat breaks out along the back of my neck and drips across my brow.

"What's wrong?" Oomka asks, looking up at my face suspiciously.

"Nothing," I reply quickly.

Several minutes later—Oomka lashed to my back like a weird Siamese twin—we set off in the direction we've agreed must be south. Still preoccupied by my strange vision, I'm not paying attention to where we're going, just treading along through the forest. Without many of his organs, Oomka is very light, but he clicks the power switch of his gun on and off and squirms.

"You're wasting the batteries," I snap, looking over my shoulder. His face falls, and the clicking sounds stop.

We trudge along in relative silence for a while before he starts picking at his teeth. Why someone with two thirds of his body missing would be worrying about his teeth is beyond me. He's slurping and sucking and scraping the enamel with his finger. I bite my tongue and say nothing, although I feel like smashing his open ribcage into a tree.

* * *

It seems like hours have passed, but the sky is still light when the forest begins to thin slightly, and we enter a clearing. I raise my gun, stepping back under the cover of the trees. Distinct signs of the recent passage of a large Jeremy—probably a tyrannosaurus, by the looks of the prints—mark the clearing. A strong smell of meat hangs in the warm, sticky air.

"What's going..." Oomka begins. I elbow his open ribcage sharply. He falls silent, but I feel him straining to peer over my shoulder.

In the center of the clearing is a great mound of earth, easily recognizable as the domicile of a larger Jeremy. During the most recent attack on a Jeremy village, all the buildings and structures were razed to the ground, leveled and burned. Nothing but plastic ruins remain in the war field, so I have never seen a dwelling up close. It looks so humble, so modest, with round, latticed windows, and a small fern garden framing a walkway to the door. It doesn't seem to reflect any of the characteristics of the savage, blood-thirsty beasts that must have constructed it.

Oomka has managed to turn himself enough to see ahead of us. He gasps and whispers, "What the fuck?"

Curiosity overcomes me, despite the potential danger. I need to explore this home. I need to see inside it. Untying Oomka, I drop him to the ground.

"Stand watch," I say.

"But…" he begins to protest.

I walk away. I hear him grumble and shift at the edge of the clearing as I move across the fern garden.

We have plenty of ammunition, not to mention the element of surprise if the building is occupied. I brace myself outside the entrance, standing between two huge, well-manicured hedges. I seek my familiar state of peace and detachment. I'm not shielding myself from fear or anxious nerves this time, but from a strange, child-like excitement.

Slowing my breathing, I lean my whole body against the massive door, and it swings open.

The majority of the wall space of the domed structure is composed of shelves upon which scores of large books are stacked, pictures in metal and wooden frames, vases, plates and cups. It looks just like a house in the village, only larger, with less furniture. Jeremies, I suppose, don't really need furniture. One glance around tells me the house is empty, although the smell of meat is strong. I walk around the interior. There is just one room with a huge, vaulted ceiling. The architecture is beautiful. From the outside, the home is simple, like a large sandy hill, but inside, crisscrossing beams and tiled floors indicate the Jeremy are just as concerned with the aesthetics of their architecture as the monks.

* * *

Then I see it. In the center, lower than the rest of the floor: a nest. In the nest are eight or nine eggs the size of beach balls. My heart pounding in my ears, I cross the floor and kneel beside the nearest egg. Without thinking, I reach out a shaking hand and place it on the stony brown surface. I yank my hand back. It's warm. I feel like my skin has just brushed the beginning of the universe. I imagine the infant dinosaur, curled up inside the egg, harmless and vulnerable, barely conscious, in need of protection and, in a flash, I know I cannot encase these eggs.

I am about to stand and turn back to the door when a little shuffle of movement a few feet away makes me leap back. In my excitement and wonder upon entering the house, I hadn't even checked for smaller Jeremies hiding in the dark corners. My first thought is that it must be a raptor. I cry out in surprise and swing my gun around in the direction of the movement. But it is a baby. A newly hatched, infant dinosaur. The movement had been the raising of its speckled head. The rest of its body is curled in a tight ball between two other eggs, half-shielded by a fragment of its old shell. It's about the size of a dog, soft and fat, clumsy and wide-eyed.

Oomka will have heard my cry. He's probably dragging himself across the clearing now. Although I know there is no way I can logically defend the nest or persuade him not to destroy it, I kneel down beside the baby dinosaur and reach out a shaking finger.

Its small, scaly nose extends, nostrils quivering curiously. I imagine that when our skins touch I will see a flash of images—all the monks this dinosaur will later kill, all the villagers it will devour, all the children it will dismember, all the men, friends and family members it will gun down and destroy. But when its nose touches my finger, nothing happens, except it nuzzles up against my hand, placing its whole head in my fingers and licking my wrist affectionately with a small, bluish tongue. My heart pounds in my ears.

* * *

I leave the house.

Oomka doesn't ask about the interior, or my yell of surprise as I reattach him to my back. I think he is just glad to get away from the place.

At one point during our return to the monastery, we talk about the possibility of a Jeremy village close to the house. "We should send a party back," he eventually says, in a tone that implies he wonders why I have not said it first.

"It was deserted," I say. "Nothing has been there for months."

Chapter Four
The Monastery

Back at the monastery the next morning, the helicopter-sized gongs in the dormitories awaken me. The gongs create pressure-blasts of sound movement as they ring, vibrating the floors and walls and shaking sleepy-eyed monks from their straw mats. I rise with the overwhelming desire to speak with the elders.

The sun has not yet risen, and the monastery is the purplish color of molding fruit. Monks stumble around like zombies, heavy-footed and battle-weary, some with bones protruding at odd angles, thick bandages shielding the majority of others from the crisp morning air.

Distant pterodactyl cries sound eerie in the mostly silent bustle of the monastery common. I feel a rush of intense rage, then sadness.

Unbalanced and confused, I amble through the overgrown grass toward the makeshift tent of the elders. The second tower had been bombed several weeks ago with huge barrels of explosives made from the deadly combination of starfruit and the dinosaurs' digestive juices, launched over the outer walls by iguanodons. It had been the first attack on monastery soil in twenty-five years.

The second tower was the traditional dwelling place of the monastic elders, and was one of the largest of eight buildings in the compound. Immediate inquiries were launched as to the possibility of a breach of security, or an informant to the outside. How, without direct knowledge of our oligarchic system of government (we had previously been sure that the dinosaurs knew little to nothing about our way of life) and a tip as to where the leaders would be sleeping, would the Jeremies have known to hit the second tower?

Once, the eight buildings of the monastic complex were

each assigned a unique and holy purpose. Now, most of them house the remaining villagers. One is dedicated to limb-re-assignment surgeries, and the other remaining building, the second tower, had, until recently, housed the temple proper and the quarters of the elders.

Chapter Five
The Oft Retold History of
The Venerable Elder Zohar

In the first days of the Jeremy, one of the elders, Elder Zohar, then just a monk a little older than myself, had been involved in one of the most re-told and recounted battles in the history of the monastery.

Back then, most of the forest still teemed with the Steve. Steves were the product of the union of the meditative energy of the monks and the badgers of the forest. The thoughts produced by the monks were most often inclined to manifest as cloudy, indistinct forest creatures. Usually these meditative cloud-beasts wandered jubilantly into the forest as if conscious and accepting of their temporary state. Once in a while, the strong, negative thoughts of a particularly disgruntled monk would take form and go on a rampage, but, thankfully, the badgers steered clear of these creatures, who typically faded to nothing without ever meeting in union to produce a Steve.

The Steve had once been the most common and abundant creature in the mountain forests. They were shy, but not unsocial, and, when coaxed by kind words, they allowed themselves to be pet and caressed. To those they deemed to be of the most even, transcendent temperaments, the Steve spoke, sometimes at length.

The wisdom of the Steve was said to be the most peaceful and natural of all wisdoms.

They were, after all, the product of an immaculate union: human meditation—absolute purity of thought—and the perfect, innocent, wild nature of the forest's most noble beast: the badger.

Even when Zohar was young, the Steve would converse with him freely. Among his favorite were a small fish-headed cat with huge white wings and soft opalescent eyes, and another with the body of a rhino and the head of a rat. *Fish-cat* and *Rat-head* were the names that Zohar, as a young monk, had given them. There were other Steves that came to speak with Zohar, but Fish-cat and Rat-head were his two oldest and dearest friends.

Those two had taught him remarkable things: secrets of the cognitive world and many interesting facts about outer space, to which both had often traveled. But one of the most useful things the Steve had taught Zohar was a magic kung-fu which only he could practice and teach to no other. Many of Zohar's fellow monks were angry and jealous when they saw him practicing the magic kung-fu, and he refused to teach them the secrets the Steve had given him.

Zohar's loyalty to the Steve caused many other monks to dislike him, and Zohar spent numerous hours wandering alone through the forests meditating, sending cloudy beasts out into the undergrowth to copulate with the badgers.

In his lonely wanderings, Zohar learned much about the mountains and the dense forests that surrounded the monastery. He grew familiar with the villages, often staying with his villager friends late into the night, talking and thinking. He knew every secret pathway and every tree like each were his ancestors.

When the first signs of something amiss manifested in the forest, it was Zohar who noticed them long before any other monk. Zohar went to the elders and told them he suspected something was wrong, but they did nothing. They were too busy and thought Zohar was odd for spending so much time alone and away from all the other monks.

Zohar confided his fears to Fish-cat and Rat-head. "Fish-cat, Rat-head," he said as they sat together one day on a log. "I sense something wrong in the forest. There are no new Steves. The sky is always dark and cloudy. There's a strange smell in the air, like meat, and I've heard no birds singing. I haven't seen a badger in a week."

Fish-cat and Rat-head seemed to look at each other brief-ly. It was hard to tell because one had the head of a fish, and the other's head was so tiny on its massive body that it could hardly turn its head at all.

Before responding, Fish-cat licked its paws with its fish tongue and blinked its milky eyes. "Soon we will be leaving," it said.

"Zohar, the days of the Steve are ending," Rat-head said in a low, rumbling voice. "The Steve cannot survive what is to come."

Zohar, his worst fears confirmed, could do nothing but stare at his knees. He thought about his two best and only friends leaving him and the forest forever. "Where are you going?" he asked. "Can I come, too?"

"No," said Fish-cat. "We won't be far."

This didn't make Zohar feel any better. He felt betrayed and scared for whatever was coming. And worst of all, he could hardly imagine a world without the Steve.

But that world wasn't far from him. In a matter of weeks, the Steve had disappeared without saying a word or leaving a forwarding address. They hadn't even packed up their houses or sold their possessions. It was as if they had all just stopped what they were doing and walked out of the forest together.

The loneliness of Zohar was great.

Then the Jeremy attacked.

The first attacks seemed to be solely for the purpose of feeding. They barged into villages in the early spring— smashing houses and tromping gardens—and snatched up all the people they could reach in their huge, razor-filled jaws. After each attack, they withdrew to some secret hiding place no one could find.

The villagers were being eaten by the handful. Villagers that Zohar knew and loved, and only Zohar seemed to care.

He went to the elders and said, "We must do something! We must find a way to protect these villagers!"

But the elders were still too busy, and they thought Zohar probably had something to do with the disappearance of the Steve. They didn't want to talk to him at all.

Enraged, disappointed, hurt, Zohar said goodbye to the elders, packed up all his worldly possessions and left the monastery. Outside the walls, villagers crowded around the door, pleading to be let in for fear that the dinosaurs would eat them. Women and men shoved their children toward Zohar helplessly.

The tents and makeshift shacks leaning against the wall had multiplied since he had been outside the monastery last, and it worried him. He felt a rush of rage and anger. Rage at the elders for not allowing these villagers to take refuge behind the walls, rage at the mysterious carnivorous dinosaurs with a taste for villagers, but especially rage at the Steve for not telling him how to fight back the monstrous beasts, or even why they were here.

All the time Fish-cat and Rat-head had spent rambling on about magnetic force and gravitational pull and the supernovae-ing of stars, they could have prepared him instead for this fight, or armed him with the knowledge he needed to survive. If they hadn't wanted to teach him, they might have at least convinced the elders he was not mad. They might have at least warned someone who had some power and influence, someone who could mobilize the monks and protect the villagers.

Zohar apologized profusely to the men and women huddled against the red walls. "I'm sorry. So sorry," he said. "I've done everything I can."

An old man stood as Zohar passed the disappointed, forlorn faces of the villagers. "But you're running away!" he said, gesturing to the pack of belongings on Zohar's back.

"I must. I've got to try to find the Steve. They can't be far."

The villagers scoffed and shook their heads. "The Steve left us all, left us to be eaten! We need to stand together," the old man said, and then pointing at the monastery's towers:

"You have shelter for the women and children. Well, we have the men, strong men with weapons we saved from the wreckage of our houses. We can fight together. Forget the Steve."

"It's no use telling me," Zohar replied, almost impatiently, but trying not to be rude. "I've already told the elders. They just won't allow it. They don't want the fighting."

The old man's eyes flashed. They were wide and dark. "We must fight," he said.

Zohar rubbed the bridge of his nose. The sack of all his worldly possessions was heavy on his back. It was mostly full of the femurs of his ancestors. A family tradition. All together, he had thirteen femurs. Zohar placed them on the sand in front of his feet, wondering how he might respond to the old man's statement.

He did not think fighting was the answer, and knew there must be a way to defeat the Jeremy without violence, without conflict, through peace and reason, through thought and strength of mind. He just wasn't sure what that way was, exactly. He wanted to tell all of this to the man, to all these people, but couldn't find words to make it sensible. He just knew he had to find the Steve. The Steve knew; they had an answer. They would tell him where the dinosaurs had come from and how to send them back and end the bloodshed.

Three small children were playing in the ferns where the edge of the forest met the monastery wall. All giggled secretively, and Zohar sighed. In the silence of this pause, the somewhat distant sound of heavy falling feet, rustling and breaking branches became audible. The sound grew nearer very fast, and, in a moment, it seemed just behind the green cloak of the forest. The villagers stopped their quiet babbling; the three children in the ferns looked up at their parents with large, round eyes, but did not move. Then, without warning, a giant crested head swung out of the forest and closed around all three of the children with one deft swoop.

A woman screamed.

The dinosaur swallowed the children without chewing. A greenish tongue flicked out of its massive jaws, and it roared mightily, head thrown back in triumph.

Remembering the magic kung-fu the Steve had taught him, Zohar sprinted toward the massive roaring head and, with a single kick, sent the dinosaur sprawling. But the kick only angered it, and it clambered back to its feet, shaking with rage. It roared again. The villagers cringed and huddled closer to the wall. Fear did not enter Zohar. He breathed deeply and waited for the dinosaur to move.

Villagers screamed and cried. The beast smiled at Zohar and charged.

What came next has been retold and recounted so many times that it has attained legendary status in the monastery.

Zohar crouched low to the ground and sprang right into the open mouth of the charging dinosaur. Rows of dagger-like teeth on the lower jaw severed his legs, but Zohar didn't flinch. He wedged himself between the mandible and the skull of the dinosaur, and, following a mighty explosive yank, tore the dinosaur's head off its body. The villagers were silent and scared.

They thought Zohar was dead. Zohar, too, almost thought this. But then he pulled himself up onto the severed head of the dinosaur. He was soaked in reptilian blood, and his legs were about seven feet away from him. They had been cut off directly below the pelvis.

Zohar reached into the esophagus of the dinosaur and pulled out the bodies of the three children, one after the other. They were dead, but at least they were no longer in an esophagus.

Now, Zohar knew what the old man had said was true. They had to fight. But even after the awe-inspiring kung-fu of Zohar defeated a dinosaur outside the very walls of the monastery, the monks still refused to engage the Jeremy.

Luckily, doctors in the infirmary had two spare hands, severed at the wrist during a game of racquetball. In the first of what was to become a myriad of brilliant reassignment surgeries, they immediately fitted the hands to Zohar's pelvis. Zohar was able to walk on his new hands within days, an unprecedented recovery. But significantly slowed by the movement of ten small fingers instead of two big legs, Zohar was forced to stay in the monastery rather than go out in search of the Steve. He eventually succeeded in convincing the elders to allow the villagers to take refuge inside the walls. Angry and heartbroken by the Steve's desertion, Elder Zohar disobeyed the instructions that Fish-cat and Rat-head had given him regarding the magic kung-fu, and he taught every monk that would listen how to practice it. It wasn't long before he forgot about looking for the Steve altogether and turned the considerable powers of his mind toward fighting the Jeremy.

Chapter Six
Take the Elephant Gun

Elder Zohar is the most respected and revered elder. He is also the oldest, but not because he is very old. Dinosaurs have eaten most of the other elders.

It is Elder Zohar who sits in the makeshift temple-tent when I enter. Well, he may actually be standing. It is hard to tell because, in standing mode, his fingers raise him only about three inches above the ground.

His back is slightly bent. His smooth, shaven head glimmers in the candlelight. I feel bad disturbing his prayer, so I linger at the back of the tent and wait for him to rise. I am only there a moment before a low voice says, "Please, come sit by me."

I tiptoe toward him and kneel at his side. His lower fingers un-flex, and he rests on his palms. He doesn't turn to face me, but stays in this hunched position, bowing slightly toward the rough-hewn gray stone idol with its glimmering golden face. "You seem troubled," he says after several full minutes of silence.

"Yes," I respond, things flickering through my mind like it's fast-forwarding the last three months: Chip's dismemberment, the battle last night, the pterodactyl's tears, Oomka's ribcage catching us as we tore through the sky, the slender body between the trees, the house, the baby dinosaur and the look on Oomka's face when I told him nothing was there.

"I heard news about Oomka," Elder Zohar says, his tone conversational. "They'll be able to give him a leg from the knee down."

I nod, my throat choked by the things I feel compelled to divulge.

After several more minutes of silence, Elder Zohar turns his face toward me. His skin is unlined and youthful, his eyes bright and penetrating. I look at them for only a moment before flicking my eyes back to the idol. "You are feeling uneasy," Elder Zohar says. "Pray, meditate and converse with your spirit."

I nod again, my body close to exploding with words I can't quite form. Another minute goes by. Finally he says, "Take the day, walk in the south fields. Bring an elephant gun and some extra ammunition."

Elder Zohar flexes his thumbs and rises onto the tips of his fingers without another word. I watch him go, wanting desperately to call out. But, in moments, he has scuttled out of the tent, the door flapping lamely in the breeze behind him.

Feeling worse than when I entered the tent, I leave several minutes after Elder Zohar.

The sky is still dark and stormy when I step outside. It seems to reflect my conversation with the elder. I consider my odd behavior, and my body seizes up with sudden embarrassment and anxiety. But I decide it best, after all, to take the elder's advice and go to the armory for an elephant gun.

The elephant gun is fitted with a tall, stainless steel, eyeball-like periscope that extends above my head for a full, elevated, 360-degree view. Extra ammunition is stored in barrels by the doors to the armory. I seize a few elephant gun cartridges. The large plastic capsules are warm in my hands.

In the south fields—once brimming with vegetable gardens, rows of wheat and rice, heads of cattle and flocks of sheep that speckled the hills in the distance—everything is flat and silent. When the Jeremy came, all the crops and livestock had to be moved inside the walls, as the dinosaurs' frequent rampages around the monastery had crushed and destroyed most of the crop. I could not remember the taste of fresh vegetables, although once, in my extreme youth, I must have had an abundance of them—as all young monks did— but in the last twenty-five years, the paltry, shade-stunted vegetables we had been able to produce had to be cooked, softened and blessed before consumption.

Things like vegetables were the easiest to forget. What was more difficult was forgetting the freedom and child-made hugeness of the land outside the monastery, the exquisite peace of wandering through forests unmarred by death and made warm and quiet by the presence of the Steve.

Due to my young age, I had never spoken to a Steve before they disappeared. I had glimpsed them several times on forest walks, but was confused and curious that everyone seemed so sad about their disappearance. I did not feel the coolness, or the subtle changes in the direction of plant leaves. I did not feel the absence of badgers.

In the south fields, I sit in the tall grass with the elephant gun over my knees.

I think about the end of days, the explosion of the center of the planet, the old man and the old woman, and if they will ever meet.

I think about how they must be lonely, about how they never search for each other, about how hopeless and disbelieving they are that a companion lurks just out of sight.

Some infant dinosaurs frolic in the overgrown wheat some distance away. Often, baby dinosaurs play here. We watch them from the walls of the monastery, but don't shoot them because they are just out of range. I wonder if this is why Elder Zohar sent me out here. If he really did know what was troubling me and wanted me to see these infant dinosaurs frolicking in the overgrown wheat, like children, awkward, clumsy and in need of protection.

But he had sent me with an elephant gun and extra ammunition. My stomach lurches uncomfortably.

* * *

I am gazing through the periscope from my low position in the wheat when a flash of movement in the corner of the sight catches my eye. I swivel the periscope around a bit and adjust the lens. Near the baby dinosaurs, a tall, slender form watches from the trees. I recognize this shape immediately. It's the one I saw before we found the dinosaur house, between the trees in the heat-waving forest.

It's certainly a dinosaur. But I don't recognize the species or any of the features. In fact, it's like nothing I've ever seen, in physical aspect or in dress. This dinosaur wears a pinkish robe, similar in shape and proportionate length to our own monk robes. No weapons are slung across its chest, no guns or blades clutched in its claws. I have never seen anything so incongruous.

But strangest of all is the shape of its body. No plates or spines or spikes mark its back, no knobby reptilian skin-warts. Its bluish-gray skin looks smooth and leathery. Its snout is flattened, like a bill, and it has large teal eyes.

A whole new species of dinosaur, just as Chip had said must exist. I'm so amazed I can barely register what I'm looking at. I need to see it closer. I need to know it. I feel so sure I should touch this dinosaur—be close to it and, if possible, speak with it. I'm barely able to disconnect myself from the periscope for fear I might lose sight of it forever.

I drop the gun and scramble, half-crawling, through the wheat. For the first few yards the dinosaur continues to stand still at the edge of the forest, watching the baby dinosaurs play. I know a triceratops or a stegosaurus is somewhere close by, supervising the infants. I veer to the left through an old fence and scurry along the rows of empty stalks.

As I near the dinosaur, she (for I am now sure it is a she) turns casually and begins to walk back into the forest. I want to cry out as fear stabs through me, but I know I would only reveal myself to the babysitter in the trees. So I run faster, tearing through dead plants, my heart pounding, feeling my robes rip and snag on thorns and protruding branches.

When I reach the edge of the forest, she is nowhere to be seen. All that remains to indicate her presence is a faint, fresh-cut tomato scent. I inhale deeply.

This is not the typical smell of a dinosaur, but it can only be her smell; it is so airy and light. I run up the mountain, following the path of the scent on the breeze, praying no other dinosaur will intercept me.

Soon enough, I hear footsteps up ahead. But as I approach somewhat noisily through the undergrowth, the footsteps stop, pause and start again, quicker. She must sense she is being followed.

I run to keep up, catching flashes of bluish-gray limbs and wafts of tomato scent as my feet pound away beneath me. Trees and branches whip my face and bare arms. Suddenly, I lose the trail of the dinosaur.

I continue in the direction I am heading, but find no sign of her. I stumble into a large clearing in the forest, legs aching. I clutch my sides, breathing heavily. Here, the forest floor is awash in tiny yellow flowers floating in a sea of pale green grass. Standing like ghosts all across the field: the jagged remains of long-since exploded plasticized dinosaurs. Spines and skulls lay in random piles or curl like barbed wire from the statues. The yellow flowers lap against flesh-colored plastic like waves. Across the field: a flash of blue.

"Wait!" I call, my first utterance rolling over the somber graveyard field like merry-making, seeming perverse and insensitive.

The dinosaur stops. She looks straight at me. The muscles of my stomach tighten like I'm going to be sick.

"Wait," I say again, not moving for fear of frightening her. "I don't want to hurt you."

She blinks her huge round eyes, the color and the texture of a tropical sea. Little splashes of light play in them like sun on waves. I want to swallow, but the lump in my throat is too big. We stare at each other across the plastic corpse-casts of Jeremies. She looks about to flee, but then I feel my arm reach out toward her.

We are across the field from one another, but this gesture seems to make her pause. She looks around at the plastic exoskeletons, her face seeming pained, although, being unaccustomed to reading the expressions of dinosaurs, it is hard for me to tell.

"We don't want this to happen," I say, not knowing why I'm speaking, or even quite what I'm saying. "*I* don't want this to happen. But I don't understand why…" My words trail into silence.

She blinks again slowly, eyes sparkling, and again I smell the powerful, tomato-y bitterness of her, like fresh growing things, like life.

She folds her claws in front of her chest. Her eyes flicker to the ground. "Neither do I," she says. Her voice is clear and calm. "It's a shame and a waste."

My heart pounds. I can't believe I'm speaking to a dinosaur.

She takes a step forward, and so do I.

"What is your name?" I ask, taking yet another step.

"Petunia," she replies, and I think I see the hint of a smile on her bill-like face.

"Where do you come from?" I ask.

"The top of the mountain." She has taken another step forward now as well. Her steps are much larger than mine.

"Why have I never seen you?" I ask. At the same time, we both seem to realize the strange weight of this statement.

"We don't fight with the other dinosaurs. We are different."

"Oh," I say. "Right."

"I have to go." She looks over her shoulder. "I'm expected. I'll be missed."

"No, wait," I say once again. Taking several more bold steps forward, I reach out my hand. I expect her to step back, but she doesn't. Instead, she reaches her long clawed arm toward me, and the very tips of our fingers touch. "Meet me here tomorrow," I say.

She squints down at me; her eyes flick to the tips of our fingers.

I pray she doesn't draw back her hand. "Meet me here,"

I repeat, deliberately, strongly, like an order.

Finally, she nods, pulls away. Our fingers disconnect.

"Meet me tomorrow," I say again.

She whirls around and trots off into the trees, disappearing in a matter of seconds as the steep incline buries her in leaves.

* * *

There are low clouds in the sky, still gray and ominous, as I turn and head back to the south fields.

The chase must have gone on much longer than I had thought, because it seems to already be getting dark. I feel exposed and vulnerable now, walking in the forest without a weapon. I haven't been outside the monastery walls without a gun in my hand since the age of seven. As I walk, the shapes in the trees and the gray sky and the fast-coming darkness all seem menacing. I think of fashioning a spear, or something out of a tree branch, before going on, but I don't want to waste any more daylight.

* * *

As I descend the mountain, a column of smoke becomes visible through a break in the trees, out toward the monastery. I stop. In the absence of my footsteps, I hear distant roars and explosions.

Another attack.

I shiver, cold sweat erupts all over my body, and I sprint as fast as I can through the undergrowth. Several seconds later, my foot catches on an exposed root, and I fly through the air, landing in a crumpled heap in the dirt. Staggering to my feet, I am overpowered by the nauseating smell of meat. Jeremies. Close.

I don't have the elephant gun.

I am scared.

I continue running, each leaping footfall skidding in the soft, mossy dirt. The sky is darker. Suddenly, a flash of red light from near the monastery.

The forest thins. I near the edge of the field. The infant dinosaurs that had been playing there have gone and, with them, their much more threatening babysitter. I should have encountered at least one watch post, but no one has called out to me. They are all fighting. Or dead.

Trying once more to shield my mind from a creeping sensation of panic, I surround my sweating body with stars and galaxies, all spinning around and elongated as if I am seeing them through glass. The stars speak to me: "Don't worry, monk, you are not a physical body. You are only a series of still images conjured into existence by three objective perceivers. They make you. They draw and project you. No Jeremy can hurt you. No dinosaur can eat you. You are not a physical body." But my suspended body is muddy, so I know it exists. "Fuck you!" I yell at the stars and galaxies, and they withdraw.

I still don't have the elephant gun.

What am I going to do when I reach the battle? Can I sneak around to the southern field and pick up the elephant gun? That's ridiculous. It's lying flat in a field of tall wheat stalks. It'll probably take me until morning to find it. And the battery will be dead. And it looks as if it's rained down here, so it'll be wet. I swear aloud a few more times. If Jeremies are sitting on watch, they'll have already heard me stumbling down the mountain for the last fifteen minutes. The smell of meat intensifies.

I hear the sounds of cannons firing and trees splintering in front of and behind me now. Explosive shots light up small areas of conflict under the forest canopy. I see the massive head of a tyrannosaurus roaring, shots being fired from some monks at the knee-level of a stegosaurus with a huge battle-axe. Bits of the forest are illuminated by burning corpses, mostly monks, some villagers. I pass a Jeremy, half-encased in plastic, beside one flaming corpse. He screams in pain as the flames lick his encased bottom half, melting away the plastic.

I have slowed my pace. Individual fights rage throughout the underbrush. I am almost caught in the crossfire of a close-range shooting battle. I duck to the ground at the last second. Both Jeremies are encased. I run past the cheering monks without stopping or acknowledging their calls.

I think I catch a glimpse of Oomka hopping on his single central foot through the trees, but it could be some other monk. Up ahead, a tree is on fire. The flames shed light over the immediate area. Plastic dinosaurs litter the forest floor. Flesh and bones are spread around too, the obliterated remains of monks.

I don't have the elephant gun. I don't have any gun. I don't even have a knife. There are roars and gunshots and sounds of screaming from every side.

This attack must have been huge, one of the largest in years. I pick up my pace again and sprint toward the monastery walls.

I pass three separate defense lines around the monastery. The first is recovering from a brachiosaurus attack. Farther down, a pile of cleanly severed limbs tells me that pterodactyls have been here with their samurai swords.

The lines grow disordered as I approach the doors. Medics run close to the walls, harvesting useful limbs from piles of monk flesh.

Suddenly, something whizzes past my face, a loose rotating saw blade. It ricochets off the wall and slams into my side. It stops against my spine, but has already severed my arm. A medic runs toward me. I see him pick up my arm. I fall to the ground.

* * *

I am on an island in the center of the planet. Rocks shaped like trees are everywhere, and on the ground, miniscule trees shaped like rocks. I am treading on the soft rock trees with my bare feet.

I think I am alone. I think I am very old. My hands are curled up and wrinkled. I feel content. Fireflies swarm high above me. They make a sound like electric lights or an idling engine. Then I am floating over the island, drifting lazily between the leaves of the tree rocks, dragging my toes through the yellow glowing sun bar of fireflies. They kiss my toes, and I laugh.

I feel a tug on my arm and look down to see Petunia reaching up into the sky. Her hand is wrapped around mine. She is pulling me down. I am in her arms. I feel as if a bluish-gray cloud has encased me.

Petunia is very old as well. She is stooped, her soft leathery skin wrinkled and pockmarked. She smiles warmly at me. Her face is familiar and comforting. I am in her arms, and she walks with me toward a house in the tree rocks. Above us, the fireflies are beginning to descend, one by one, until they fall in a torrent, a deluge of fireflies. They swirl through the air as I push the door open in front of Petunia. We enter our house.

So do the fireflies.

They light on every surface. They land on high-backed chairs and a little fireplace. They land on a worn-out rug and a big couch with soft cushions. Petunia's arms, wrapped around my body, are covered in fireflies.

We are so old.

We feel very tired all of a sudden, and so we lie down together, on the old worn-out rug, surrounded by dancing fireflies. We fall asleep gazing into one another's eyes.

Chapter Seven
Surprise Attack

It has not been very long. It is still dark. The sky is a dusky orange-ish gray. A shadowy line of treetops flickers with lights from fires in the south fields.

Several firefights still rage in the distance. I hear gunshots and the ping of plastic cartridges discharging.

My temples throb, and my first thought is that the medics have harvested the rest of my limbs and left me for dead on the battlefield. To my relief, I find most of my appendages still intact. I sit up. My right side feels strangely light. Blood trickles in a steady stream from the place where my arm had been, and a large triangular chunk cut out of my side exposes some muscle, ribs and an organ I can't identify.

Columns of smoke continue to rise from the forest north of the monastery. No other monks are in sight; at least not any who could be resurrected by the medics.

It's probably best to get inside. I clamber to my feet, feeling unsteady.

Inside the monastery walls, I'm told by seven separate monks to get to the temple tent. They push me, like they don't think I'm capable of moving myself. I allow my body to be hurried along, still slightly dazed.

Oomka is inside the tent. He looks better than he did the day before yesterday. The medics have attached a leg from the knee down to his sternum. He is a little taller than Elder Zohar now. I look at him curiously, but he doesn't say anything. His eyes are on the ground in front of Elder Zohar, who rests on the knuckles of his hands, looking at a hand-drawn map in front of him.

"You're here," he says. "Finally." He scratches his chin and then points to the map, his small, beady eyes darting up to look at me after a moment. His gaze sweeps over my missing arm, but he doesn't say anything about it.

"You and Oomka are to take an attack party and approach the site from the east. The rocky ground there will hide you until you're practically on top of them."

Oomka still looks deliberately at the map, his brow furrowed.

"Sorry, on top of who?" I ask.

Elder Zohar's eyes narrow, boring uncomfortably into mine. I turn my eyes away just as he opens his mouth to speak. "The Jeremy nest," he says. "Elder Bradley and I agree that we cannot risk the nest being inhabited. It may have appeared deserted, but that is no guarantee the animals are gone for good. Best to destroy it before anything can return."

"Wait," I say without thinking, without knowing what I am going to say afterwards.

Elder Zohar's gaze narrows again, and his eyes dig into my skull, filling my brain cavity with searching, grasping, multi-jointed, tentacle-like fingers. I feel as if he knows what I am thinking. But that's impossible. I see Oomka's eyes flicker up to mine, then back down to the map. I am thinking again about Chip, inside the stomach of a stegosaurus encased in plastic. I am suddenly revolted with myself. "Alright," I say, "but I need a gun."

The Elder nods.

* * *

The mountain seems eerily silent after the remnant snatches of battle have faded behind us. No one speaks as we march up the mountain, led by Oomka on his new leg, hopping with a strange determination I have never seen in him. He does not fidget. I watch as familiar portions of forest pass beneath our feet. The hike up the mountain is taking a significantly shorter time than the hike down, despite the fact that we are now laden with plastic ray guns and flame throwers and are traveling up a steep incline.

Before we even catch a glimpse of the clearing in the trees, we hear the sounds of muffled voices.

The house is in sight, its little shuttered windows thrown open to the night air. Smells of cooking and the now-obvious sounds of baby Jeremy squealing and stamping around inside hit the party some twenty feet outside the clearing. The three other monks exchange significant looks. Beads of sweat form on my forehead despite the coolness of the night. I feel a hotness rush through the empty space where my right arm had been, like it is still attached.

At a sign from Oomka, the three other monks rush forward. Oomka vaults himself over the rocky outcrop behind which I still crouch. Using the gun in his hand as a second leg, he hobbles after them quickly.

Flames explode from the guns of the three monks closest to the house, bursting through a window. Screams from inside. The door swings open. The face of a Jeremy appears. Before the Jeremy can register the presence of attackers, Oomka has encased it. Another is close behind. The Jeremy shoves its encased mate through the doorway carelessly, shotgun in hand. Two explosive shots ring out. One monk lets out a scream. A gaping, badger-sized hole through his torso, he falls to his knees, dropping the flamethrower, which ignites the tall grass in the clearing. His body collapses upon itself, and he disappears in the flaming grass.

I leap over the rock, imagining I am leaping into the ocean. Instead of this murderous tyrannosaurus wielding a fourteen-foot shotgun loaded with badger-sized buckshot, blue whales circle slowly around me, singing softly, their music low and soothing, but pervasive, everywhere, filling the water, wrapping itself around me like a cashmere cocoon.

High screeching sounds emanate from the house. A pillar of flames reaches up above the tops of the trees.

Oomka takes aim at the second tyrannosaurus and shoots, but his shot misses by an inch and lands on the roof of the smoldering home. The plastic bubbles and smokes. One of the other monks aims his flamethrower at the Jeremy. Oom-ka takes another shot, this time making contact. The Jeremy is frozen mid-scream in flesh-colored plastic, jaw stretched wide, the shotgun aimed at Oomka's head.

It is suddenly quiet. The sound of crackling flames is the only sound now. I walk around the home, searching the white and yellow flames and thick black columns of smoke for signs of life. I am on the opposite side of the burning home from Oomka.

There is a rustle in the tall grass. I kneel.

It is a baby Jeremy, crawling soundlessly, clutching at the grass and dirt with its tiny front arms, dragging its legs along behind it. Its eyes are huge in its skull, and beneath the sound of the house burning I hear it breathing short, heavy breaths.

The remaining monks follow me around the house.

I stand and crush its skull with the heel of my foot.

It folds so easily, like a deflating basketball. The body stops moving.

I think of Petunia. My lost arm throbs painfully.

* * *

The next morning, I awake before the other monks. In the hall at breakfast, I listen to them as they mutter to each other. They say that someone is telling the Jeremy how to break through our defenses. The attack last night was the most devastating in years, and so soon after the last one. It doesn't make any sense; something is different, they say. There's a spy. They glare around with suspicious, furrowed eyebrows.

I swallow.

With a pang of sadness, I imagine what Chip would think if he knew where I had been yesterday. Then I think of my heel crushing the soft skull of the baby dinosaur. I feel nause-ated. But the Jeremy, as Chip would have said, are not people;

they are not monks. They are animals, beasts, dinosaurs.

Petunia.

A red rush of confusion and pain. I feel imaginary blood pulse through the imaginary fingertips of my left arm. I cannot bring myself to say Petunia is not a person, is not a monk, is an animal, a beast, a dinosaur.

I feel I am going insane.

The air in the hall is oppressive and thick.

I wonder where Oomka is, and how he is doing after the attack last night.

I glance around the hall one last time and walk out into the commons. Oomka is probably sitting by himself somewhere, away from the other monks.

Sure enough, I find him on a bench by the rock garden. He is significantly shorter now, his half-leg attached right at the sternum of his remaining ribcage, which has been mostly bandaged shut. He is sort of balancing on the knee with his head bent upward a little.

He doesn't look too bad. The wounds are obviously still healing, but they are much less terrifying than they had been, and not at all the worst this monastery's monks have faced.

Still, he looks up at me somewhat sullenly as I approach. "Where were you yesterday? Are you alright?" he asks, eyeing my missing arm, but not with pity or concern.

"Oh, it's nothing," I say, brushing a hand across the remaining portion of my shoulder. It itches, but it doesn't exist. "How's your leg?"

"It's great," he says with almost-convincing bravado.

"It's just going to take some getting used to," I say, trying to smile kindly while taking a seat on the bench behind him.

"The battle was really something last night," Oomka says. "Probably the most Jeremy we've ever seen at once."

"It looked awful. I got there toward the end, but I'd lost my weapon."

We fall awkwardly silent.

"What were you doing yesterday?" he asks after a moment.

"I was on an assignment from the elder," I lie. Well, it isn't exactly a lie. It *had* been Elder Zohar's suggestion that I visit the south fields.

I think of Petunia, her gray-blue skin and her smooth, soft bill, the electric feeling of her hand touching mine.

Oomka does not respond.

"I've got another assignment, well, for this morning..." I say hesitantly, wondering with a sinking feeling if, after the battle last night, Petunia will still be waiting in the clearing in the south forest.

Oomka nods. "That's fine. I can cover for you on watch. There shouldn't be any trouble today. After last night, you know."

I nod and stand to leave.

"Bye then," Oomka says, his eyes narrowing slightly as if he has something else to say, but he doesn't say anything.

"See you tonight."

"Be careful," he says.

"You too."

I walk out of the monastery, unarmed, for the second time.

Chapter Eight
Fragrant Dinosaur Skin

Petunia stands in the center of the clearing. In a circle around her, a spot of sunlight shines down from the stormy sky. It's as if she's glowing.

I make some noise as I step into the little meadow, so I don't startle her. She turns around and looks at me with her huge, heart-swallowing eyes. My stomach churns again. I feel suddenly conscious of my body, my missing arm, my bare, leathery feet.

"What happened?" she asks, eyeing my arm-less shoulder with her brow raised in an expression of concern.

"Oh nothing," I respond quickly, brushing the wound as I had done when responding to the same inquiry from Oomka.

She bends low, her face close to mine. My heart is beating so loud it echoes in the space between us, like someone snapping a rubber band.

Her clawed finger brushes the still oozing wound, and it is then I hear her heartbeat, too—the sound between us is the meeting of the two beats, synchronized perfectly.

As before, Petunia and I have the same thought at the same moment. Her face is close to mine, her clawed finger lingering just above my shoulder. Our breaths seem like those of one body. Her eyes are wide, their glassy surfaces sparkling with the reflection of the yellow flower-strewn meadow grass, like multitudes of winking stars in a brightening teal-dawn sky.

Finally, Petunia breaks our silence. "I want to show you something." She bends low to allow me to clamber onto her back where I perch between her massive shoulder blades. I hold tight to her neck, and she races off into the forest.

I have never experienced anything quite like this sensation of movement. Wind rushes past me and around me, lifting my robes and chilling my skin. Leaves and branches whip my legs. I try hard to hold on, but my single arm won't reach all the way around her neck, so I grasp at her leathery hide.

"Am I hurting you?" I ask, speaking loudly in the wind.

She seems to chuckle a little as her wide steps carry us up the mountain. "No," she says, turning her head around a little so I can see one round, teal eye. Her face is crinkled in a smile. "Your hand feels nice."

A rushing wall of green comes into focus as we slow. We're nearing the edge of a steep cliff. When we stop, her heart beats loudly beneath me. I lay my palm, trembling, against the side of her neck and feel blood course through her veins in bursts.

At the edge of the tree line, we look out to where the undergrowth thins and the beginnings of a steep rocky slope become visible.

"You can get off," she says, and I slide reluctantly from her back.

She catches me with an arm and lowers me to the ground. I walk toward the precipice. "I wanted you to see them," she says. She is smiling again. I am sure of that now.

I peer down into the little valley below. The view is beautiful. We are almost all the way up the south face of the mountain. There is no sign of humans, monks, or Jeremy for miles in every direction. A fork of lightening far in the distance lights up the gray horizon.

At first, the valley appears covered in a thin mist, but, as I gaze down at the treetops, I see them quiver and shift—sparkling, thin wisps of smoke shivering in and out of existence like a badly-tuned TV, some twisting around trees and diving up and down jubilantly. They remind me of something I have seen before, but I can't place the memory.

Petunia smiles. "They belong to us, to the trachodon. Other dinosaurs who come to the top of the mountain to live with us send them out, too. They only last a while, but they're beautiful, aren't they?"

I realize these are thoughts—trachodon thoughts—much smaller and less solid than the thoughts of monks. They look like the thoughts of children, but they *are* beautiful, like she said. Questions erupt across my mind, but I am captivated by the wisps of thought flickering like clouds of shifting fireflies.

I smile at Petunia. "They're amazing," I say. I wish I were large enough to carry her, to wrap all the way around her and lift her up into the air with me. I wish I were a huge pterodactyl with a wingspan longer than the entire monastery, so I could take her up in my giant claws and fly away from the forest, over the mountain, across the ocean. As we look at each other, there's no doubt in my mind that she's thinking the same thing. My mind feels calm and soft, like a ripe peach. I feel as if nothing could hurt me, like the whole rest of the universe is made of soft peaches, too. And what can soft fruit do to soft fruit? I place a hand on Petunia's knee, the highest place I can reach. The place where our skin meets is like a warm pillow. "Let's go," she says after we have stood there for a few minutes. "That storm is coming our way."

Glad to be on Petunia's back again, I clamber up with her help and snuggle into her fragrant dinosaur skin. "Your eyelashes tickle," she giggles. I squeeze her tight with my whole body, and she laughs as we begin the descent.

* * *

After bidding Petunia goodbye and arranging to meet here again tomorrow, I tromp noisily through the forest. The soft peachiness of my mind seems to cushion the sounds, making everything fuzzy and indistinct. I'm lost in the memory of Petunia's body.

It has begun to rain, and I hear the pattering on the canopy above, but only the occasional drop makes it through the roof of trees.

Chapter Nine
Sharing a Dream

Early in the morning, I pace the hallway of the monk's dormitory. Through a window the sky is starless, but not yet gray with pre-dawn light. My eyes feel raw and sore.

I have been awake all night, reading and re-reading all of the major texts on the Jeremy for some hint, some allusion to the trachodons or their thoughts, anything that would explain what Petunia had shown me.

Eventually, I decide to go down to the temple-tent and meditate. No one will be there this early, so I can avoid the company of other monks. Even the calm, rhythmic sounds of their nighttime breathing make me anxious.

The commons are as quiet as the dormitory. I cross the sandy paths, listening for dinosaurs in the distance. On the mountainsides to the south, small lights from campfires flicker through the trees. I can't tell whether they are the fires of the monks or the Jeremy. There are no sounds and no other sign that living things still inhabit the valley. Everything is still.

When I enter the tent, I sense immediately that I am not alone. My heart pounding in my chest, I feel imaginary blood coursing through non-existent fingertips again. The shrine is dark, the only light coming from a single candle lit in one corner. A shadow low to the ground shifts a little, and I search around for something to throw, something to stab, but, before I can locate a weapon, the shadow shifts into the light.

It is Elder Zohar.

I exhale a huge sigh.

His eyes and partially open mouth are three black holes in the light. I am speechless, relieved and a little revolted. He kneels on the knuckles of his lower hands.

"Come closer. You are not interrupting anything," says

Elder Zohar in a low, tired voice.

I kneel in front of the shrine beside him once more, feeling anxious and worried. Perhaps coming to the temple-tent had not been a good idea. After a moment, Elder Zohar speaks in his breathy voice. "You have been troubled these past days."

I am silent. I can't think of a response to this statement. Not one I should divulge to an elder, at least.

"Do you have anything you wish to tell me?" he continues.

As before, thoughts rush into my mind, questions that maybe Elder Zohar would be able to answer.

We sit in silence for a moment more. Outside the tent, a bird sings. It is the first living sound of the morning, apart from the sound of Elder Zohar's voice, if that can be said to have been a living sound. Grayness will seep in through the rough canvas of the tent. The giant morning gongs will be struck. Monks will rise. More fighting. More carnage. In only a few minutes.

"Actually," I say, my voice loud in the empty temple tent. "Actually, yes. Well, I have a question."

Elder Zohar inclines his bald head attentively.

"I wanted to ask you if...well...if the Jeremy have thoughts. I mean, do they make thoughts, like the monks used to?" I ask carefully.

Elder Zohar is silent for a few minutes, but I can tell he is contemplating my question. I already feel relieved. Elder Zohar, in his wisdom, will be able to offer a suitable explanation for what I have seen, for what I am feeling, an explanation that neither the books of the library, nor my own meditations could provide.

"The Jeremy are not monks," Elder Zohar says after a few minutes of silence. "They are not people; they are animals, beasts, dinosaurs. They have no thoughts." He turns toward me. His eyes are black holes again, but I see a reflective sparkle at the center of each lightless pit. "You already know this."

My heart pounds again. Petunia's face. The skull of the baby dinosaur. Chip's last screams. Anger and revulsion and pity and sadness and, most of all, confusion shakes me. I make to stand up without response, but the elder places a warm hand on the remaining piece of my shoulder.

"Go where you will today," Elder Zohar says. "Walk in the forest." He sighs deeply and pats my shoulder affectionately, as if he understands my thoughts. "Finish your business there, but remember what I have told you, and remember what you already know."

I am confused by this advice. But I nod and lift the flap. I walk several paces and stop. I hear voices back in the tent. At first, I think Elder Zohar is simply praying aloud, but then there is another voice. I step lightly around to the back of the shrine.

"I want you to follow our friend today, watch where he goes," Elder Zohar's voice says.

"Do you think he is the spy?" With a stomach–plunging chill, I recognize Oomka's voice.

"I cannot say just yet, but follow him, report only to me, tell no one where you are going."

Rage. Sadness. I rub my arm stump and head toward the armory.

I figure it is less suspicious to be seen sneaking out of the monastery armed than unarmed. I will take the elephant gun.

* * *

The sky is lighter, a dusty pink. The storm clouds that have hung low around the mountaintops have receded. Bare yellow rays of sun shoot up from the horizon now. I swing the elephant gun over my back and start out across the south fields.

If Oomka is following me, he won't be able to hide himself well in the open field, recently ravaged by battle. Bits of ground still smolder gently. I glance quickly over my shoulder and see Oomka hop behind the leg of a plastic tyrannosaur. Oomka may be many things, but stealthy is not one of them. I wonder why the elder would send Oomka, of all the monks, to tail me.

I'll lose him easily in the labyrinthine mountain forest. Only I know where I am headed. I quicken my pace upon entering the trees. Oomka still hops on his lower arm about a hundred yards behind, using his two original arms as crutches.

I cut through the forest diagonally, heading in the opposite direction of my destination. After fifteen minutes of jogging through undergrowth, I am convinced I have lost him. I stand still in the forest, listening to the blood pounding in my ears and the distant sounds of pterodactyls. There is no sign of Oomka.

Satisfied, I head toward the clearing.

I will see Petunia.

I will climb up onto her smooth dinosaur back and hold her closely with all of my remaining limbs.

Rays of sunshine shimmer in the dusty green and yellow air of the forest. My mouth is dry and my hand is hot and sweaty. I feel warm and bright.

* * *

Petunia follows me. I hear her massive crashing dinosaur steps a few yards away. It must be tedious for her to walk this slowly behind me, but I don't know how to explain where we are going.

I turn to face her. She is closer than I expect. My heart leaps in surprise, and the sudden closeness overwhelms me. I want to bury my whole body in the curve of her neck. Instead, I run a hand over her lowered bill. "I wanted to show you this place. It's where my friend Chip is… well, it's where he died." I gesture through the trees, and Petunia looks past me. She straightens up a little. Her head rises out of reach.

We are actually quite close to the monastery, but few

people ever come this way. There are no wanderers in the forest anymore.

Towering above us is the plasticized corpse of a stegosaurus. The Jeremy was huge, even for its species. It has not exploded its shell because it was not fully encased. The yellowish bone of its back leg is visible, protruding through the flesh-colored plastic. On its face is a look of rage, I imagine, although its plastic features are hard to read. I glance back at Petunia as I lay a hand on the leg of the stegosaurus.

"He's in there," I say. "He was my best friend."

Hot tears gather in my eyes, but I look up and blink them back. I don't want to cry in front of Petunia.

I can't explain to her what it meant to lose Chip. That it was like losing the most sensible part of myself. That it had been worse than the loss of my arm, worse than being doubted by all the monks.

Petunia seems to scowl. It takes me a moment to realize she isn't scowling in confusion or anger. Instead, she's sad like me.

"I don't understand why this is happening," I say again.

"It won't go on forever," Petunia says. I don't understand this.

"Why don't the trachodons help us? If there are other types of Jeremy," I pause, looking to see if this word has offended her, but she stares unblinkingly into my eyes. "If there are other types of dinosaurs, why don't they help the monks? We could stop all of this. We could fight."

Petunia rubs her chin and sighs, "They're waiting for a sign. That's all I can tell you."

I feel frustrated and angry and can't seem to detach myself here, sitting beside the stegosaurus that ate Chip.

She leans forward and lifts me up in her dinosaur arms. I curl myself around her neck, holding her the best I can in my condition. She sits against the leg of the stegosaurus and rocks me back and forth. Little spots of sunshine drift in and out of the trees, highlighting bits of forest, bits of Petunia, bits of the stegosaurus that ate Chip. I feel light, like I am being carried out to sea.

Petunia's skin is warm and soft. I am inside of it, like Chip is inside the stegosaurus. It is dark because my eyes are closed, but points of light shine through from outside. I realize the light is coming through two windows. I didn't know Petunia's body had windows. I call out to Chip, but he doesn't answer. I knock on one of the windowpanes. No answer there, either.

I can't see any way out, but don't feel trapped. I feel enclosed and enveloped, peaceful, like I am wrapped in the skin of a peach, like I am wearing a huge badger-skin coat, like I am swaying in the ocean.

Through the window, I see Petunia and me sleeping together beneath the stegosaurus. Petunia looks beautiful and serene. Her eyes are closed, but on her face is a ghostly smile. I think she is dreaming. I wonder if we are dreaming together. I hope we are.

Then, suddenly, like steam erupting from a teakettle, two wisps of smoke emerge from us. They entwine and merge so quickly I can't tell whether they were ever separate at all. The thoughts swirl around above us, growing increasingly opaque with each turn.

Within seconds, they have become a thick, grayish blob hovering in mid-air. The blob seems to open its mouth, and I hear a shrill cry. I feel myself, the self outside of Petunia, shiver. The blob plunges into my head.

I awake with a start. Petunia curls herself a little tighter around me. I am wrapped in the warm folds of her skin. My head throbs. As I stir, Petunia turns to look at me.

"Were you dreaming?" she asks.

"Yes," I say, rubbing my temples. There is a large lump on my forehead. I prod it with a finger, and stars explode in my eyes. "I have a terrible headache." I rest my throbbing head against Petunia's stomach.

"I wonder what time it is?" she says, looking up at the

sky. "I need to get back to the top of the mountain before dark."

I want to tell Petunia that I was inside her; I want to tell her about the grayish blob and the windows, but, before I can speak, there is a rustle in the trees a few yards away. Petunia sits up abruptly. I slip to the ground.

"What was that?" she whispers.

I grab for the elephant gun and aim it at the rustling. "Maybe a badger, or a squirrel," I say, praying I'm right.

"It seemed larger," she says, standing up.

"Oomka?" I whisper, almost under my breath. A horrible chill settles over the forest.

A one-legged shape bounds out of the trees, back toward the monastery. I can't shoot the elephant gun. I look up at Petunia.

"Who was that," she says. It doesn't seem like a question.

"Not sure. Get back to the trachodons," I say before touching her outstretched dinosaur hand one last time.

She seems to sense the unease in my voice and bounds away without another word.

* * *

My head pounds; the lump swells. It is now roughly the size and shape of an orange. My skin stretches painfully around it.

I don't have time to worry about my head. I must get back to the monastery.

Not far from the watch-line, I catch a whiff of meat. I stop my trudging, stand still and listen. I hear a faint crackle, like a fire burning, but no other sound. I approach the watch-line from the enemy side. I'll spot the monks in just a moment. They should be right ahead, but there is no sound, no call.

They must have noticed already. I continue walking, carefully, aiming the elephant gun in front of me. The first thing I see is a burning bush. Beneath the bush: a half-cooked human arm and a pile of eyeballs.

A few feet away, I find another bit of human, from the same or a separate body, I cannot tell. I hurry west toward the next watch post.

Similar people chunks litter the area.

I break into a sprint.

* * *

At the third watch, I find a whole half of a monk weeping on the ground. I can't stop to help.

At the adjacent post, there is only a discarded gun. I pick it up. The hand of a monk still clutches it. The rest of the monk is missing. I dislodge the hand and tuck the ray gun into my robes.

* * *

The fifth watch site is completely abandoned. A tree nearby has been severed about 20 feet up, the work of tyrannosaurs, no doubt. It seems like five simultaneous attacks. No warning. I can't feel the prickling flood of panic I think I should be feeling. I just know I need to get to the monastery. Now.

Chapter Ten
Mighty Birth

The attack came on so silently and so quickly; no one had any warning or time to prepare.

The south fields swarm with Jeremy. Monks send flocks of pigeons over the walls carrying small plastic bombs. Plastic-encased Jeremy dot the battlefield. The sky is thick with deafening roars and explosions, mixed with the quick pattering of bullets and the squelching sound of guns discharging. I run across the open field, firing into the walls of Jeremy on either side. All around me, dinosaurs freeze in plastic shells. Several small squadrons of monks are in the fray, cutting lines through the massive attack force. This is by far the most Jeremies I've ever seen in one place.

Leaving a line of dead dinosaurs behind me, I slam into the double doors of the monastery. A raptor chases after me. I aim the ray gun toward him and hear a tiny *splooch*. I'm out of ammunition. I throw the gun at the raptor, but it sidesteps around it. I curse aloud and brace my body for the impact.

The raptor leaps from about three feet away. It lands on my chest and knocks my body backwards onto the ground. Its jaws open with a screech. I hit it in the snout, but catch my hand in its mouth as I scramble back. Teeth scrape the skin of my wrist and arm down to the bone. I raise my injured fist again and punch the raptor in its right eye. It cries out in pain and leaps back. I search around wildly, blood pouring from my wound. The raptor shakes its head like a wet dog, rattled but not destroyed. I need a weapon. Quick.

I snatch a branch up from the ground and brandish it like a sword. The raptor bends low, opens it mouth and screeches loudly. Three other raptors a little ways behind it look over with interest. Two of them hold a monk while the third punches him in the stomach.

The raptor in front of me is about to charge. I don't think my stick will do much, even if I can get in a good hit. Then someone yells. I risk a glance over my shoulder, and the raptor charges. The call has come from a monk behind the monastery door.

"Get your stupid ass in here!" the monk screams. I sprint toward him. The raptor is gaining. I feel its hot breath on my ankles as I squeeze through the door and help the monk slam it behind me.

"That was close," I say, dropping my stick in the sand.

"No shit," the monk says. He wipes his brow with the foot attached to his left arm and glares at me. "Elder Zohar wants you. Now."

This hostility seems a bit out of character, but I shrug it off. "Where is he?"

"In the temple-tent, fuck brain," the monk snaps, gesturing violently toward the tent before turning back to the stairs up to the wall.

I cross the commons. Monks run across it carrying loads of ammunition and big cages full of pigeons and squirrels. Fire rains down from the sky. I feel I should have a weapon in hand, but don't think I have time to stop by the armory. Elder Zohar's request seems urgent.

When I enter his tent, I find two elders sitting, praying before the great gold-faced idol. Elder Zohar glances over his shoulder as I enter. He rises onto his fingertips. He lifts one of his lower fingers and cracks the knuckle against the carpet. "Seize him!" he says. The other elder turns around and looks at me. I think he's scowling, but it's difficult to say, as half of his face is a thigh.

I whirl around. Three monks flank the tent entrance. Two of them rush forward, grabbing my arm. The third monk is Oomka. I look to him for help. "Oomka, what's going on? Help me!"

"No one will help you now, traitor," the thigh-faced elder says in a muffled voice, and then, turning to Oomka, "What's wrong with his face?"

"We know where you have been going; we know what you have done," says Elder Zohar, ignoring the thigh-faced elder. "I knew something was troubling you yesterday, but I never suspected this. I thought that killing a few Jeremies would cure you of whatever was ailing you. Now, I know that it is a deep sickness of the mind."

"What?" I say, horrified and confused.

"How could you do this to us?" says Oomka in a quaking voice. I struggle to turn my body to look at him, but the two monks holding me painfully by the shoulders jerk me backward.

"What do you mean? I don't understand what's happening. What do you think I did?"

"It's no use playing dumb, you traitorous nag," says Elder Zohar. "You were seen giving confidential information to a Jeremy." He spits on the floor.

For a second, I'm speechless. I look to Oomka.

"I followed you," says Oomka, his eyes wide and sad now. "I saw you with that Jeremy. I'm sorry. I had to say something."

He *had* seen me, but what had he said? Was Petunia safe? Would the peaceful enclave of trachodons at the top of the mountain be massacred? Panic. It doesn't matter if the monks plan on torturing me or killing me. There is no one to warn the trachodons.

"No, you don't understand!" I shout. "It's not what it seems!" Looking directly into Elder Zohar's eyes, I say as calmly as I can, "They're peaceful; they're a species we don't know about, and they make thoughts, like the monks used to do. Believe me, I've seen these thoughts."

Elder Zohar scoffs and spits again. "Take him to the third tower and lock him up. Don't let anyone in the building."

The two monks who have my arm yank it backward, hard. "And send a group of monks up the south face of the mountain to the top. Let's bomb these fuckers before they come down and join the party," Elder Zohar says to the thigh-faced elder.

Tears. Huge, sloppy, childish tears pour down my face as the monks drag me across the commons toward the third tower. I can't stop the flow.

My giant face welt is still swelling. I feel it pulsing on top of my head. How the hell am I going to reach Petunia? I have to warn the trachodons. I have to save them. I have to save Petunia, burrow down to the center of the earth with her and take refuge on an empty island. It is the only way. We can grow old there, like in my dream, and be free of all this war and bloodshed and sadness.

* * *

From my window, I see the battle raging below. It looks hopeless. The Jeremy swarm the walls, so many of them, piled on top of each other in a rolling mound of spiny, reptilian flesh. My head throbs.

Huge cannons mounted on the tops of plesiosaurs fire giant flaming moths that flap over the monastery, raining fire down on the monks. A blast shakes the tower.

I figure there are a few possibilities now, and none of them sound promising: Either Jeremies break through the monastery walls and kill me, monks kill me for betraying them, or the giant mass on my head expands until it explodes and kills me.

Two tyrannosaurs near the southeast corner of the wall chip away at stone with the huge white femurs of their ancestors. No one protects that corner of the wall. It looks like a flaming moth crash-landed on the section, a twenty-foot circle of ground charred and black around it.

I have to do something. But my head throbs. I sink down under the window, still sobbing unconsciously, although the huge mass, which is now about as big and round as my entire head, prevents my eyes from excreting any real tears.

I try to return to the soft peach place Petunia had created in my mind. But it seems so far off, buried deeply beneath my immediate pain and horror. I reach, swimming through blackness, and there is a teal light above me, and a door with a little gleaming handle in the pupil of an eye. It is Petunia's eye.

I reach for the door and turn the handle. Petunia's eye is furnished like an old Victorian cottage. It looks like the room in which we grew old together, in my dream. I walk to the couch and bury my face in the gaudy floral fabric. It is rough but warm. My face welt has shrunken to a small lump again, and I hear the sounds of dishes clinking in the kitchen, then a soft voice calls, "Will you peel some of these potatoes for me, baby?"

I raise my head and look through the door to the kitchen. Petunia stands in a pink apron, beating eggs. She smiles warmly and gestures to the kitchen table where a little basket of potatoes sits near an empty metal bowl. Three baby dinosaurs run in and out of the room, laughing and screaming. "Walking feet, boys!" Petunia chides.

I sit at the table and begin to skin the potatoes into the bowl. I watch Petunia, rolling dough on the island. She looks up and sees me watching her. "What's up?" she giggles.

"Nothing," I say, shaking my head and looking at the potato in my hands. "You're beautiful."

She laughs and rubs the bottom of her bill, leaving a little smear of flour behind. I laugh, too.

* * *

There's a huge crash from the battlefield. I snap back to reality and gaze out the window. Jeremies have broken through the monastery wall. Monks flee from the huge tyrannosaurs stomping in at the front. No one fights back. No one shoots. Everyone runs.

A lightening bolt of pain, and the welt on my head cracks

open. Screaming, I fall to my knees. White splotches of agony cloud my vision. I try to rush back to the eyeball house, but can't see anything. Everything is washed out. I must be dying.

There is a ripping sound as something huge crawls out of my head. A leathery wing unfolds, covered in sticky yellow mucus. It flips around, and then the whole thing drops to the floor.

It's a pterodactyl.

It looks at me. It cocks its head and squawks.

I rush toward the pterodactyl and clamber onto its back. "Take me to the trachodons; take me to my Petunia!" I tell it.

It squawks obligingly and spreads its wings.

Chapter Eleven
Everyone Holds Hands

We soar through the air, as high as the tower and gaining altitude. The monks below are little mice. The tyrannosaurs are little cats.

We are far above the monastery now. The mice become mosquitoes. The cats become crane flies.

The forest sweeps past beneath us like a soft green carpet. I hug the pterodactyl that sprang from me. It lets out a happy squawk and turns to wink at me. I stroke the bright orange crest on it head. "Thank you," I say.

* * *

The trachodon village is in a clearing like the one where I first spoke to Petunia. Small yellow flowers adrift in a bright green sea. I am reminded of Petunia's eyes. Suddenly, she is running toward me.

There are no monks, no plastic-encased dinosaurs. I let out a huge sigh of relief, but there is no time to rest, no time to hug Petunia with my whole body.

"Quick!" I yell as she approaches. "The monks are coming with guns!"

Other trachodons are listening. Some scream. A mother grabs her child by the hand.

"What's happening? We heard explosions," Petunia says, grabbing me up in her arms and holding me against her chest like she did in my dream. My feet dangle twenty or so feet off the ground.

An older-looking trachodon peers out of a door nearby. "Everyone calm down," he calls across the clearing. Upon his approach, he bends low to peer at me. "Tell us what's going on, young man," he says.

Petunia sets me back on the ground. I tell the gathering crowd of trachodons what is happening at the monastery. My pterodactyl squawks a few times as if to confirm my story. The trachodons nod and gasp.

There is silence across the gathering. They look at each other. The older trachodon looks from Petunia to me. She is crouched down; we are holding hands.

"George," says the old trachodon suddenly to another, "go quickly and fetch the Steve. Everyone else," his chest swells as he looks around the clearing, "the time has come. This is the sign for which we have been waiting. Prepare for battle."

I whirl around. "Battle?" I ask. "And you have the Steve?"

Petunia scoops me up in her arms again and puts me on her back. "I'll explain later," she says, hurrying off in a crowd of trachodons. "Just keep quiet up there for a bit."

Suddenly, trachodons rush toward one building near the opposite end of the clearing from which I entered. They run past us, armed with metal plates and chain mail, carrying spears and swords. Two others push a tall wooden catapult. My pterodactyl follows us on foot. He squawks a little as he runs awkwardly.

"What's going on?" I ask. "Where's everyone going?"

"To the monastery. We're going to help you beat the Jeremy, once and for all," Petunia says.

"We don't stand a chance!" I yell, my throat constricting in panic. "You can't! The monks will think you're on the side of the Jeremy!"

"It's alright," Petunia says, looking around as she hurries toward the armory. "The Steve will help us."

* * *

Petunia and I race down the mountain, surrounded by trachodons in suits of armor, carrying steel swords as long as city buses. Strange creatures of various size and shape run alongside us. I sit, perched above Petunia's shoulder blades. Her head is enclosed in a shiny helmet. She carries a giant mace.

The Steve carry no weapons. I wonder how they will be able to help the trachodons. My pterodactyl, however, was given a samurai sword, his species' preferred weapon. He flies behind us, squawking excitedly. His squawks give me a little more confidence.

As we near the rear of the battle, we see small groups of monks still fighting in the field, but things seem to have gotten worse since I escaped. The monastery is overrun. Buildings burn.

The south fields are so thick with plastic dinosaurs that the trachodons must spread out to weave through them. Once clear, they plunge their swords into Jeremies, taking them by surprise. Luckily, as Jeremies fall around them, the last groups of monks fighting recognize that the trachodons are on their side.

We make our way steadily toward the monastery walls. Jeremies farther up seem to realize something is happening at the rear of the battle.

Trachodons, no longer able to take the Jeremy by surprise, begin to fall under heavy machine gun fire. Blades explode from the guns of the stegosaurs. Petunia ducks, raising her hands to shield me. The blades zip over our heads, slicing another trachodon in three. Petunia doesn't flinch.

Even amidst all this carnage and death, I'm amazed at her bravery.

A stegosaurus—two massive iron cannons mounted on either side of its scaly back—approaches rapidly. Trachodons scatter. Cannons fire. Everything around us erupts into flames. Petunia dives to the side just in time to avoid the blast, but other trachodons are caught in the blaze, screaming in agony as their dinosaur flesh bubbles and burns. My pterodactyl flies ahead of us. He squawks jubilantly as he slices the head from a plesiosaur carrying a long bow. The plesiosaur's paddle-feet twitch on the ground, and my pterodactyl rises up into the air triumphantly, sounding his victory with a mighty squawk.

I notice, with a rush of anger, that the Steve cower behind the trachodons on the edge of the forest. Assorted furry and fishy faces watch the battle anxiously.

"I thought you said the Steve would help us!" I yell to Petunia. She is grinding the head of a raptor into the ground beneath us.

"They need energy; they're gathering strength!" she calls back, whirling around to throw the mace into an approaching triceratops' face.

Looking back, I notice that not every Steve stands around watching. At the back of the group, several are gathered in a circle. Steves are creatures made of energy. I realize they must need the destructive energy of the battle to act. All the same, I wish they would hurry up. A curious yellow glow seems to encircle them; but maybe I am imagining it.

Suddenly, I feel the need to do something, too. Hiding on Petunia's back makes me feel useless, so I slide down into the fray.

At once, and only inches from my body, a trachodon clubs another triceratops over the head with a battleaxe. Triceratops blood splatters me. The liquid is hot and sticky, and I feel sick. Still, I lunge toward the detached forearm of a fallen monk and grab the flamethrower lodged beneath it.

I whirl around and torch an approaching tyrannosaur. The flames don't stop him. Thick steel plates cover his front and sides. He slashes the three towering spikes strapped to his head at me, catching me in my armless side. I feel a stab of pain as they connect with my spine, and I soar up into the air.

I can do no more than gasp before I land squarely in the arms of a trachodon, who had apparently dove onto the ground to catch me. It is the old trachodon to whom I had spoken on the mountaintop.

"Get back to Petunia," he says.

I decide it's best to listen to him. He drops me into the crumpled wheat stalks of the scarred field, and I search for Petunia.

She's nowhere to be seen. There's only a dense cloud of blood, flesh and severed limbs, dinosaurs and monks flying in every direction.

I scream her name, but Petunia doesn't materialize from the mass. A huge clawed foot stomps down close to me, and I scramble out of the way as three more feet stomp by, leaving gaping holes in the field. It's another stegosaurus, laden this time with one half of a rotating saw-blade apparatus. It runs in a circle, unable to move the machine on its back without a partner. The whirling blade catches trachodons, severing them in half. Monks try to duck under the blade as it passes; some are cut in half as well.

As I watch, holding the flamethrower, unable to move, the stegosaurus spins around and heads back toward me. The glistening silver blade is feet away. I can do nothing but wait, so I flatten myself in the mud, covering my head with the flamethrower. Suddenly, a huge clawed hand snatches me.

The hand throws me up into the air. As I twist around above the battle, I see Petunia beneath me, leaping over the stegosaurus, plunging the sharpened base of her mace into the Jeremy's eye. Then Petunia snatches me out of the air and slams me hastily onto her back.

I can see across the battlefield again. Trachodons are losing ground; Jeremies have overrun the monastery. In the distance, a plesiosaur hangs onto the top of the third tower, waving its green front limbs around in apparent triumph.

My stomach plunges into my toes. We are losing; perhaps we have already lost.

Petunia begins wrestling with a tyrannosaur. I cling on for dear life when, suddenly, finally, the Steve—aglow with yellow light—rush out from behind the trachodons. The lumbering, sprinting animals tear toward oncoming Jeremies through a forest of plasticized corpses. Human flesh and blood-soggy wheat squish beneath their claws and hooves.

Bullets whiz past them. Several make contact, and those bodies fall under the pounding feet of the other Steve.

Ten feet from impact with the Jeremies, a wave of cloudy, twinkling mist shoots from the glowing Steve. Those Jeremies that it hits vomit fireflies into the air, roar in agony and clutch their bellies. They drop their guns and swords and kneel, choking and gasping as the insects crawl out of their eyes and nostrils and tear past their razor-sharp teeth in swarms. Dinosaur flesh rains from the sky as bodies explode from the inside all around the monks still fighting up ahead.

The sparkling firefly mist sweeps over the field. Trachodons follow. The air glows yellow. Fireflies are everywhere. The air is too thick with them to breathe. I am choking on fireflies.

The trachodons race toward the monastery. The mist has hit the walls. Jeremies collapse all around. The Steve charge and climb the walls.

Monks run behind us, cheering and whooping. Monks drop their guns and fall into prostrations. Monks hug each other. Monks wave detached arms and legs.

Monks and Steve embrace each other. Steves kiss monks. Trachodons lift monks up into the air. Monks ride on trachodons. Monks kiss trachodons. Trachodons kiss Steves.

Monks run toward the monastery. Steves run toward the monastery. Trachodons run toward the monastery. The high brick walls of the monastic compound are piles of red-gray rubble. Smoke billows out of the windows of the remaining buildings. Scared-looking villagers crawl out of the wreckage and stare at the ocean of exploded dinosaurs. Meat and intestines cover the south field. Giant pieces of ribcage and twitching dinosaur limbs protrude from the mess. Swaths of skin and chunks of muscle are draped over the plasticized dinosaur statues.

Columns of black smoke curl up into the gray sky.

* * *

In the midst of the celebrating monks, holding one of Petunia's clawed fingers in my hand, I watch a fish-headed Steve walk slowly out of the remains of the temple-tent. The white canvas is draped over the tall idol, obscuring its face.

The fish-headed Steve carries half a monk.

No, it's not just half a monk. It's Elder Zohar.

A long sword protrudes from his chest. The Steve carrying him is crying.

Elder Zohar never went to find the Steve. His face is frozen in anger. His bald head glistens with moisture. His bottom fingers are clenched into fists, and his intestines trail behind the Steve.

Elder Zohar performed Harakiri. He is dead.

It has just begun to rain. Petunia and I are holding hands.

Epilogue
The Myth of the Great Creator

There is a story told by the monks that, at the End of Days, another age will begin. Once the earth has been split up, the pieces that once made the crust and the carpet and the wide, open, cavernous center will rejoin in a new and better order.

In this other age, monks, fireflies, Jeremy, badgers, villagers, and Steve will live together. They won't know they are together. Like the old people on the islands in the Myth of the Great Destroyer, they will wander through the forests of the reformed planet, missing each other by seconds as they round corners, or turn just a moment too late to see a passing someone in the semi-darkness.

But the forests will be full of sounds, and of life. And so will be the skies.

Herds of Steve will lounge in the sun, and millions of badgers will play together in the trees. Storms of clouds will drift up through leaves and gather in the sky, swirling around each other, everything secretly embracing.

ABOUT THE AUTHOR

Kirsten Alene lives in Portland, Oregon. Her fiction and poetry has appeared or is forthcoming in Bust Down the Door and Eat All the Chickens, Ellipsis, The Battered Suitcase, and Rivets. Visit her online at www.pterodactylsamurai.wordpress.com.

Bizarro books

CATALOG   SPRING 2010

Bizarro Books publishes under the following imprints:

www.rawdogscreamingpress.com

www.eraserheadpress.com

www.afterbirthbooks.com

www.swallowdownpress.com

For all your Bizarro needs visit:

WWW.BIZARROCENTRAL.COM

Introduce yourselves to the bizarro genre and all of its authors with the Bizarro Starter Kit series. Each volume features short novels and short stories by ten of the leading bizarro authors, designed to give you a perfect sampling of the genre for only $5 plus shipping.

BB-0X1
"The Bizarro Starter Kit"
(Orange)

Featuring D. Harlan Wilson, Carlton Mellick III, Jeremy Robert Johnson, Kevin L Donihe, Gina Ranalli, Andre Duza, Vincent W. Sakowski, Steve Beard, John Edward Lawson, and Bruce Taylor.

236 pages $5

BB-0X2
"The Bizarro Starter Kit"
(Blue)

Featuring Ray Fracalossy, Jeremy C. Shipp, Jordan Krall, Mykle Hansen, Andersen Prunty, Eckhard Gerdes, Bradley Sands, Steve Aylett, Christian TeBordo, and Tony Rauch.

244 pages $5

BB-001 "The Kafka Effekt" D. Harlan Wilson - A collection of forty-four irreal short stories loosely written in the vein of Franz Kafka, with more than a pinch of William S. Burroughs sprinkled on top. **211 pages $14**

BB-002 "Satan Burger" Carlton Mellick III - The cult novel that put Carlton Mellick III on the map ... Six punks get jobs at a fast food restaurant owned by the devil in a city violently overpopulated by surreal alien cultures. **236 pages $14**

BB-003 "Some Things Are Better Left Unplugged" Vincent Sakwoski - Join The Man and his Nemesis, the obese tabby, for a nightmare roller coaster ride into this postmodern fantasy. **152 pages $10**

BB-004 "Shall We Gather At the Garden?" Kevin L Donihe - Donihe's Debut novel. Midgets take over the world, The Church of Lionel Richie vs. The Church of the Byrds, plant porn and more! **244 pages $14**

BB-005 "Razor Wire Pubic Hair" Carlton Mellick III - A genderless humandildo is purchased by a razor dominatrix and brought into her nightmarish world of bizarre sex and mutilation. **176 pages $11**

BB-006 "Stranger on the Loose" D. Harlan Wilson - The fiction of Wilson's 2nd collection is planted in the soil of normalcy, but what grows out of that soil is a dark, witty, otherworldly jungle... **228 pages $14**

BB-007 "The Baby Jesus Butt Plug" Carlton Mellick III - Using clones of the Baby Jesus for anal sex will be the hip sex fetish of the future. **92 pages $10**

BB-008 "Fishyfleshed" Carlton Mellick III - The world of the past is an illogical flatland lacking in dimension and color, a sick-scape of crispy squid people wandering the desert for no apparent reason. **260 pages $14**

BB-009 **"Dead Bitch Army" Andre Duza** - Step into a world filled with racist teenagers, cannibals, 100 warped Uncle Sams, automobiles with razor-sharp teeth, living graffiti, and a pissed-off zombie bitch out for revenge. **344 pages $16**

BB-010 **"The Menstruating Mall" Carlton Mellick III** - "The Breakfast Club meets Chopping Mall as directed by David Lynch." - Brian Keene **212 pages $12**

BB-011 **"Angel Dust Apocalypse" Jeremy Robert Johnson** - Meth-heads, man-made monsters, and murderous Neo-Nazis. "Seriously amazing short stories..." - Chuck Palahniuk, author of Fight Club **184 pages $11**

BB-012 **"Ocean of Lard" Kevin L Donihe / Carlton Mellick III** - A parody of those old Choose Your Own Adventure kid's books about some very odd pirates sailing on a sea made of animal fat. **176 pages $12**

BB-013 **"Last Burn in Hell" John Edward Lawson** - From his lurid angst-affair with a lesbian music diva to his ascendance as unlikely pop icon the one constant for Kenrick Brimley, official state prison gigolo, is he's got no clue what he's doing. **172 pages $14**

BB-014 **"Tangerinephant" Kevin Dole 2** - TV-obsessed aliens have abducted Michael Tangerinephant in this bizarro combination of science fiction, satire, and surrealism. **164 pages $11**

BB-015 **"Foop!" Chris Genoa** - Strange happenings are going on at Dactyl, Inc, the world's first and only time travel tourism company.

"A surreal pie in the face!" - Christopher Moore **300 pages $14**

BB-016 **"Spider Pie" Alyssa Sturgill** - A one-way trip down a rabbit hole inhabited by sexual deviants and friendly monsters, fairytale beginnings and hideous endings. **104 pages $11**

BB-017 "The Unauthorized Woman" Efrem Emerson - Enter the world of the inner freak, a landscape populated by the pre-dead and morticioners, by cockroaches and 300-lb robots. **104 pages $11**

BB-018 "Fugue XXIX" Forrest Aguirre - Tales from the fringe of speculative literary fiction where innovative minds dream up the future's uncharted territories while mining forgotten treasures of the past. **220 pages $16**

BB-019 "Pocket Full of Loose Razorblades" John Edward Lawson - A collection of dark bizarro stories. From a giant rectum to a foot-fungus factory to a girl with a biforked tongue. **190 pages $13**

BB-020 "Punk Land" Carlton Mellick III - In the punk version of Heaven, the anarchist utopia is threatened by corporate fascism and only Goblin, Mortician's sperm, and a blue-mohawked female assassin named Shark Girl can stop them. **284 pages $15**

BB-021 "Pseudo-City" D. Harlan Wilson - Pseudo-City exposes what waits in the bathroom stall, under the manhole cover and in the corporate boardroom, all in a way that can only be described as mind-bogglingly irreal. **220 pages $16**

BB-022 "Kafka's Uncle and Other Strange Tales" Bruce Taylor - Anslenot and his giant tarantula (tormentor? fri-end?) wander a desecrated world in this novel and collection of stories from Mr. Magic Realism Himself. **348 pages $17**

BB-023 "Sex and Death In Television Town" Carlton Mellick III - In the old west, a gang of hermaphrodite gunslingers take refuge from a demon plague in Telos: a town where its citizens have televisions instead of heads. **184 pages $12**

BB-024 "It Came From Below The Belt" Bradley Sands - What can Grover Goldstein do when his severed, sentient penis forces him to return to high school and help it win the presidential election? **204 pages $13**

BB-025 **"Sick: An Anthology of Illness" John Lawson, editor** - These Sick stories are horrendous and hilarious dissections of creative minds on the scalpel's edge. **296 pages $16**

BB-026 **"Tempting Disaster" John Lawson, editor** - A shocking and alluring anthology from the fringe that examines our culture's obsession with taboos. **260 pages $16**

BB-027 **"Siren Promised" Jeremy Robert Johnson & Alan M Clark** - Nominated for the Bram Stoker Award. A potent mix of bad drugs, bad dreams, brutal bad guys, and surreal/incredible art by Alan M. Clark. **190 pages $13**

BB-028 **"Chemical Gardens" Gina Ranalli** - Ro and punk band Green is the Enemy find Kreepkins, a surfer-dude warlock, a vengeful demon, and a Metal Priestess in their way as they try to escape an underground nightmare. **188 pages $13**

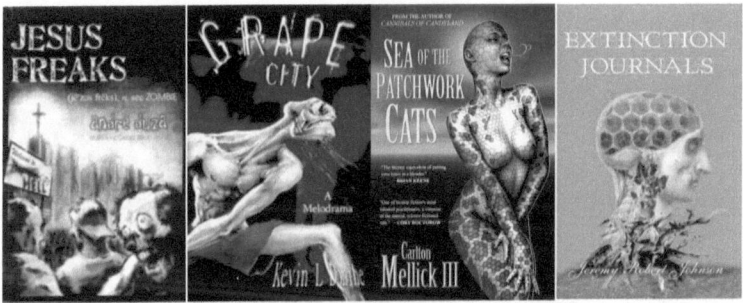

BB-029 **"Jesus Freaks" Andre Duza** - For God so loved the world that he gave his only two begotten sons… and a few million zombies. **400 pages $16**

BB-030 **"Grape City" Kevin L. Donihe** - More Donihe-style comedic bizarro about a demon named Charles who is forced to work a minimum wage job on Earth after Hell goes out of business. **108 pages $10**

BB-031 **"Sea of the Patchwork Cats" Carlton Mellick III** - A quiet dreamlike tale set in the ashes of the human race. For Mellick enthusiasts who also adore The Twilight Zone. **112 pages $10**

BB-032 **"Extinction Journals" Jeremy Robert Johnson** - An uncanny voyage across a newly nuclear America where one man must confront the problems associated with loneliness, insane dieties, radiation, love, and an ever-evolving cockroach suit with a mind of its own. **104 pages $10**

BB-033 "Meat Puppet Cabaret" Steve Beard - At last! The secret connection between Jack the Ripper and Princess Diana's death revealed! **240 pages $16 / $30**

BB-034 "The Greatest Fucking Moment in Sports" Kevin L. Donihe - In the tradition of the surreal anti-sitcom Get A Life comes a tale of triumph and agape love from the master of comedic bizarro. **108 pages $10**

BB-035 "The Troublesome Amputee" John Edward Lawson - Disturbing verse from a man who truly believes nothing is sacred and intends to prove it. **104 pages $9**

BB-036 "Deity" Vic Mudd - God (who doesn't like to be called "God") comes down to a typical, suburban, Ohio family for a little vacation—but it doesn't turn out to be as relaxing as He had hoped it would be... **168 pages $12**

  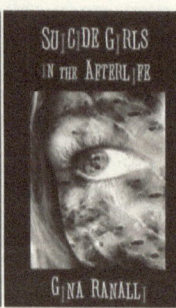 

BB-037 "The Haunted Vagina" Carlton Mellick III - It's difficult to love a woman whose vagina is a gateway to the world of the dead. **132 pages $10**

BB-038 "Tales from the Vinegar Wasteland" Ray Fracalossy - Witness: a man is slowly losing his face, a neighbor who periodically screams out for no apparent reason, and a house with a room that doesn't actually exist. **240 pages $14**

BB-039 "Suicide Girls in the Afterlife" Gina Ranalli - After Pogue commits suicide, she unexpectedly finds herself an unwilling "guest" at a hotel in the Afterlife, where she meets a group of bizarre characters, including a goth Satan, a hippie Jesus, and an alien-human hybrid. **100 pages $9**

BB-040 "And Your Point Is?" Steve Aylett - In this follow-up to LINT multiple authors provide critical commentary and essays about Jeff Lint's mind-bending literature. **104 pages $11**

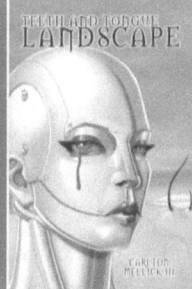

BB-041 **"Not Quite One of the Boys" Vincent Sakowski** - While drug-dealer Maxi drinks with Dante in purgatory, God and Satan play a little tri-level chess and do a little bargaining over his business partner, Vinnie, who is still left on earth. **220 pages $14**

BB-042 **"Teeth and Tongue Landscape" Carlton Mellick III** - On a planet made out of meat, a socially-obsessive monophobic man tries to find his place amongst the strange creatures and communities that he comes across. **110 pages $10**

BB-043 **"War Slut" Carlton Mellick III** - Part "1984," part "Waiting for Godot," and part action horror video game adaptation of John Carpenter's "The Thing." **116 pages $10**

BB-044 **"All Encompassing Trip" Nicole Del Sesto** - In a world where coffee is no longer available, the only television shows are reality TV re-runs, and the animals are talking back, Nikki, Amber and a singing Coyote in a do-rag are out to restore the light **308 pages $15**

BB-045 **"Dr. Identity" D. Harlan Wilson** - Follow the Dystopian Duo on a killing spree of epic proportions through the irreal postcapitalist city of Bliptown where time ticks sideways, artificial Bug-Eyed Monsters punish citizens for consumer-capitalist lethargy, and ultraviolence is as essential as a daily multivitamin. **208 pages $15**

BB-046 **"The Million-Year Centipede" Eckhard Gerdes** - Wakelin, frontman for 'The Hinge,' wrote a poem so prophetic that to ignore it dooms a person to drown in blood. **130 pages $12**

BB-047 **"Sausagey Santa" Carlton Mellick III** - A bizarro Christmas tale featuring Santa as a piratey mutant with a body made of sausages. 124 pages $10

BB-048 **"Misadventures in a Thumbnail Universe" Vincent Sakowski** - Dive deep into the surreal and satirical realms of neo-classical Blender Fiction, filled with television shoes and flesh-filled skies. **120 pages $10**

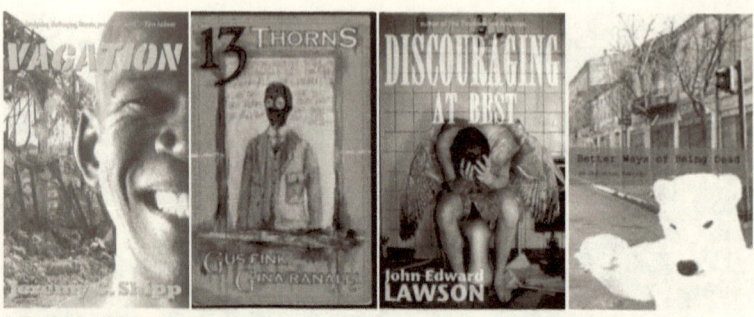

BB-049 **"Vacation" Jeremy C. Shipp** - Blueblood Bernard Johnson leaved his boring life behind to go on The Vacation, a year-long corporate sponsored odyssey. But instead of seeing the world, Bernard is captured by terrorists, becomes a key figure in secret drug wars, and, worse, doesn't once miss his secure American Dream. **160 pages $14**

BB-051 **"13 Thorns" Gina Ranalli** - Thirteen tales of twisted, bizarro horror. **240 pages $13**

BB-050 **"Discouraging at Best" John Edward Lawson** - A collection where the absurdity of the mundane expands exponentially creating a tidal wave that sweeps reason away. For those who enjoy satire, bizarro, or a good old-fashioned slap to the senses. **208 pages $15**

BB-052 **"Better Ways of Being Dead" Christian TeBordo** - In this class, the students have to keep one palm down on the table at all times, and listen to lectures about a panda who speaks Chinese. **216 pages $14**

BB-053 **"Ballad of a Slow Poisoner" Andrew Goldfarb** Millford Mutterwurst sat down on a Tuesday to take his afternoon tea, and made the unpleasant discovery that his elbows were becoming flatter. **128 pages $10**

BB-054 **"Wall of Kiss" Gina Ranalli** - A woman... A wall... Sometimes love blooms in the strangest of places. **108 pages $9**

BB-055 **"HELP! A Bear is Eating Me" Mykle Hansen** - The bizarro, heartwarming, magical tale of poor planning, hubris and severe blood loss... **150 pages $11**

BB-056 **"Piecemeal June" Jordan Krall** - A man falls in love with a living sex doll, but with love comes danger when her creator comes after her with crab-squid assassins. **90 pages $9**

BB-057 **"Laredo" Tony Rauch** - Dreamlike, surreal stories by Tony Rauch. **180 pages $12**

BB-058 **"The Overwhelming Urge" Andersen Prunty** - A collection of bizarro tales by Andersen Prunty. **150 pages $11**

BB-059 **"Adolf in Wonderland" Carlton Mellick III** - A dreamlike adventure that takes a young descendant of Adolf Hitler's design and sends him down the rabbit hole into a world of imperfection and disorder. **180 pages $11**

BB-060 **"Super Cell Anemia" Duncan B. Barlow** - "Unrelentingly bizarre and mysterious, unsettling in all the right ways..." - Brian Evenson. **180 pages $12**

BB-061 **"Ultra Fuckers" Carlton Mellick III** - Absurdist suburban horror about a couple who enter an upper middle class gated community but can't find their way out. **108 pages $9**

BB-062 **"House of Houses" Kevin L. Donihe** - An odd man wants to marry his house. Unfortunately, all of the houses in the world collapse at the same time in the Great House Holocaust. Now he must travel to House Heaven to find his departed fiancee. **172 pages $11**

BB-063 **"Necro Sex Machine" Andre Duza** - The Dead Bitch returns in this follow-up to the bizarro zombie epic Dead Bitch Army. **400 pages $16**

BB-064 **"Squid Pulp Blues" Jordan Krall** - In these three bizarro-noir novellas, the reader is thrown into a world of murderers, drugs made from squid parts, deformed gun-toting veterans, and a mischievous apocalyptic donkey. **204 pages $12**

BB-065 "Jack and Mr. Grin" Andersen Prunty - "When Mr. Grin calls you can hear a smile in his voice. Not a warm and friendly smile, but the kind that seizes your spine in fear. You don't need to pay your phone bill to hear it. That smile is in every line of Prunty's prose." - Tom Bradley. **208 pages $12**

BB-066 "Cybernetrix" Carlton Mellick III - What would you do if your normal everyday world was slowly mutating into the video game world from Tron? **212 pages $12**

BB-067 "Lemur" Tom Bradley - Spencer Sproul is a would-be serial-killing bus boy who can't manage to murder, injure, or even scare anybody. However, there are other ways to do damage to far more people and do it legally... **120 pages $12**

BB-068 "Cocoon of Terror" Jason Earls - Decapitated corpses...a sculpture of terror...Zelian's masterpiece, his Cocoon of Terror, will trigger a supernatural disaster for everyone on Earth. **196 pages $14**

BB-069 "Mother Puncher" Gina Ranalli - The world has become tragically over-populated and now the government strongly opposes procreation. Ed is employed by the government as a mother-puncher. He doesn't relish his job, but he knows it has to be done and he knows he's the best one to do it. **120 pages $9**

BB-070 "My Landlady the Lobotomist" Eckhard Gerdes - The brains of past tenants line the shelves of my boarding house, soaking in a mysterious elixir. One more slip-up and the landlady might just add my frontal lobe to her collection. **116 pages $12**

BB-071 "CPR for Dummies" Mickey Z. - This hilarious freakshow at the world's end is the fragmented, sobering debut novel by acclaimed nonfiction author Mickey Z. **216 pages $14**

BB-072 "Zerostrata" Andersen Prunty - Hansel Nothing lives in a tree house, suffers from memory loss, has a very eccentric family, and falls in love with a woman who runs naked through the woods every night. **144 pages $11**

BB-073 **"The Egg Man" Carlton Mellick III** - It is a world where humans reproduce like insects. Children are the property of corporations, and having an enormous ten-foot brain implanted into your skull is a grotesque sexual fetish. Mellick's industrial urban dystopia is one of his darkest and grittiest to date. **184 pages $11**

BB-074 **"Shark Hunting in Paradise Garden" Cameron Pierce** - A group of strange humanoid religious fanatics travel back in time to the Garden of Eden to discover it is invested with hundreds of giant flying maneating sharks. **150 pages $10**

BB-075 **"Apeshit" Carlton Mellick III** - Friday the 13th meets Visitor Q. Six hipster teens go to a cabin in the woods inhabited by a deformed killer. An incredibly fucked-up parody of B-horror movies with a bizarro slant. **192 pages $12**

BB-076 **"Rampaging Fuckers of Everything on the Crazy Shitting Planet of the Vomit At smosphere" Mykle Hansen** - 3 bizarro satires. Monster Cocks, Journey to the Center of Agnes Cuddlebottom, and Crazy Shitting Planet. **228 pages $12**

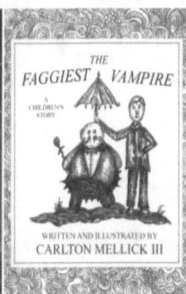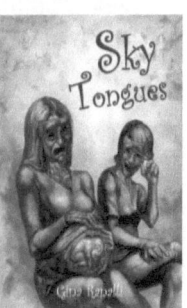

BB-077 **"The Kissing Bug" Daniel Scott Buck** - In the tradition of Roald Dahl, Tim Burton, and Edward Gorey, comes this bizarro anti-war children's story about a bohemian conenose kissing bug who falls in love with a human woman. **116 pages $10**

BB-078 **"MachoPoni" Lotus Rose** - It's My Little Pony... *Bizarro* style! A long time ago Poniworld was split in two. On one side of the Jagged Line is the Pastel Kingdom, a magical land of music, parties, and positivity. On the other side of the Jagged Line is Dark Kingdom inhabited by an army of undead ponies. **148 pages $11**

BB-079 **"The Faggiest Vampire" Carlton Mellick III** - A Roald Dahl-esque children's story about two faggy vampires who partake in a mustache competition to find out which one is truly the faggiest. **104 pages $10**

BB-080 **"Sky Tongues" Gina Ranalli** - The autobiography of Sky Tongues, the biracial hermaphrodite actress with tongues for fingers. Follow her strange life story as she rises from freak to fame. **204 pages $12**

BB-081 **"Washer Mouth" Kevin L. Donihe** - A washing machine becomes human and pursues his dream of meeting his favorite soap opera star. **244 pages $11**

BB-082 **"Shatnerquake" Jeff Burk -** All of the characters ever played by William Shatner are suddenly sucked into our world. Their mission: hunt down and destroy the real William Shatner. **100 pages $10**

BB-083 **"The Cannibals of Candyland" Carlton Mellick III** - There exists a race of cannibals that are made of candy. They live in an underground world made out of candy. One man has dedicated his life to killing them all. **170 pages $11**

BB-084 **"Slub Glub in the Weird World of the Weeping Willows" Andrew Goldfarb** - The charming tale of a blue glob named Slub Glub who helps the weeping willows whose tears are flooding the earth. There are also hyenas, ghosts, and a voodoo priest **100 pages $10**

BB-085 **"Super Fetus" Adam Pepper -** Try to abort this fetus and he'll kick your ass! **104 pages $10**

BB-086 **"Fistful of Feet" Jordan Krall -** A bizarro tribute to spaghetti westerns, featuring Cthulhu-worshipping Indians, a woman with four feet, a crazed gunman who is obsessed with sucking on candy, Syphilis-ridden mutants, sexually transmitted tattoos, and a house devoted to the freakiest fetishes. **228 pages $12**

BB-087 **"Ass Goblins of Auschwitz" Cameron Pierce** - It's Monty Python meets Nazi exploitation in a surreal nightmare as can only be imagined by Bizarro author Cameron Pierce. **104 pages $10**

BB-088 **"Silent Weapons for Quiet Wars" Cody Goodfellow** - "This is high-end psychological surrealist horror meets bottom-feeding low-life crime in a techno-thrilling science fiction world full of Lovecraft and magic..." -John Skipp **212 pages $12**

BB-089 "Warrior Wolf Women of the Wasteland" Carlton Mellick III
Road Warrior Werewolves versus McDonaldland Mutants...post-apocalyptic fiction has never been quite like this. **316 pages $13**

BB-090 "Cursed" Jeremy C Shipp - The story of a group of characters who believe they are cursed and attempt to figure out who cursed them and why. A tale of stylish absurdism and suspenseful horror. **218 pages $15**

BB-091 "Super Giant Monster Time" Jeff Burk - A tribute to choose your own adventures and Godzilla movies. Will you escape the giant monsters that are rampaging the fuck out of your city and shit? Or will you join the mob of alien-controlled punk rockers causing chaos in the streets? What happens next depends on you. **188 pages $12**

BB-092 "Perfect Union" Cody Goodfellow - "Cronenberg's THE FLY on a grand scale: human/insect gene-spliced body horror, where the human hive politics are as shocking as the gore." -John Skipp. **272 pages $13**

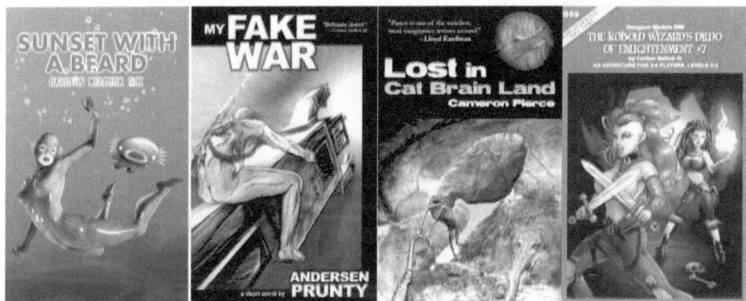

BB-093 "Sunset with a Beard" Carlton Mellick III - 14 stories of surreal science fiction. **200 pages $12**

BB-094 "My Fake War" Andersen Prunty - The absurd tale of an unlikely soldier forced to fight a war that, quite possibly, does not exist. It's Rambo meets Waiting for Godot in this subversive satire of American values and the scope of the human imagination. **128 pages $11**

BB-095 "Lost in Cat Brain Land" Cameron Pierce - Sad stories from a surreal world. A fascist mustache, the ghost of Franz Kafka, a desert inside a dead cat. Primordial entities mourn the death of their child. The desperate serve tea to mysterious creatures. A hopeless romantic falls in love with a pterodactyl. And much more. **152 pages $11**

BB-096 "The Kobold Wizard's Dildo of Enlightenment +2" Carlton Mellick III - A Dungeons and Dragons parody about a group of people who learn they are only made up characters in an AD&D campaign and must find a way to resist their nerdy teenaged players and retarded dungeon master in order to survive. 232 **pages $12**

BB-097 "My Heart Said No, but the Camera Crew Said Yes!" Bradley Sands - A collection of short stories that are crammed with the delightfully odd and the scurrilously silly. **140 pages $13**

BB-098 "A Hundred Horrible Sorrows of Ogner Stump" Andrew Goldfarb - Goldfarb's acclaimed comic series. A magical and weird journey into the horrors of everyday life. **164 pages $11**

BB-099 "Pickled Apocalypse of Pancake Island" Cameron Pierce A demented fairy tale about a pickle, a pancake, and the apocalypse. **102 pages $8**

BB-100 "Slag Attack" Andersen Prunty - Slag Attack features four visceral, noir stories about the living, crawling apocalypse. A slag is what survivors are calling the slug-like maggots raining from the sky, burrowing inside people, and hollowing out their flesh and their sanity. **148 pages $11**

BB-101 "Slaughterhouse High" Robert Devereaux - A place where schools are built with secret passageways, rebellious teens get zippers installed in their mouths and genitals, and once a year, on that special night, one couple is slaughtered and the bits of their bodies are kept as souvenirs. **304 pages $13**

BB-102 "The Emerald Burrito of Oz" John Skipp & Marc Levinthal OZ IS REAL! Magic is real! The gate is really in Kansas! And America is finally allowing Earth tourists to visit this weird-ass, mysterious land. But when Gene of Los Angeles heads off for summer vacation in the Emerald City, little does he know that a war is brewing...a war that could destroy both worlds. **280 pages $13**

BB-103 "The Vegan Revolution... with Zombies" David Agranoff When there's no more meat in hell, the vegans will walk the earth. **160 pages $11**

BB-104 "The Flappy Parts" Kevin L Donihe - Poems about bunnies, LSD, and police abuse. You know, things that matter. 132 **pages $11**

ORDER FORM

TITLES	QTY	PRICE	TOTAL

Please make checks and moneyorders payable to ROSE O'KEEFE / BIZARRO BOOKS in U.S. funds only. Please don't send bad checks! Allow 2-6 weeks for delivery. International orders may take longer. If you'd like to pay online via PAYPAL.COM, send payments to publisher@eraserheadpress.com.

SHIPPING: US ORDERS - $2 for the first book, $1 for each additional book. For priority shipping, add an additional $4. INT'L ORDERS - $5 for the first book, $3 for each additional book. Add an additional $5 per book for global priority shipping.

Send payment to:

BIZARRO BOOKS
C/O Rose O'Keefe
205 NE Bryant
Portland, OR 97211

Address

City   State   Zip

Email   Phone

www.ingramcontent.com/pod-product-compliance
Lightning Source LLC
Chambersburg PA
CBHW020730250626
47155CB00006B/2238